A M
S M

THE ESCAPED
BOOK ONE

KRISTIN CAST

DIVERSIONBOOKS

Diversion Books
A Division of Diversion Publishing Corp.
443 Park Avenue South, Suite 1008
New York, New York 10016
www.DiversionBooks.com

For more information, email info@diversionbooks.com

First Diversion Books edition June 2015.
Print ISBN: 978-1-62681-553-7
eBook ISBN: 978-1-62681-552-0

For Ja

You are an amazing teacher, mother, and friend.
I couldn't have done this without you.

PROLOGUE

The ancients knew them as the Furies, seekers of justice. Three sisters who acted as jailers, overseeing those who threatened to end humanity and feed from the souls of the innocent. Each sister wore a face of the phases of woman: Maiden, Mother, and Crone. These powerful, ethereal beings held bubbling rage, sickness, and violence locked within the deepest level of the Underworld. It is there that they made their home; in a crystal cave in the heart of Tartarus. In the light of the sugary chandeliers, their gypsum-frosted cavern shimmered like sun-kissed rain. Centuries passed while the sisters kept watch with only each other and the prisoners of Tartarus as companions.

Until, one day, love drifted down from the Mortal Realm and sprouted in the heart of Maiden...

* * *

"There are only two types of mortals," Mother sniffed as she shuffled through her large wardrobe. "The condemned and the saved." She pulled out a scarf and tossed it on the bed. It landed in a clump next to Maiden.

Maiden fingered the scarf's soft purple velvet. "But what if you are wrong? What if there are infinite types of mortals and they are more complex than they seem?"

Mother's short brown hair skimmed her shoulders as she turned to deliver a withering glance to Maiden. "How could they be? They are born and die in the time it takes for you to make even the simplest of decisions."

"We cannot blame them for having such a short time on earth. I am merely wishing to experience their world, as I have experienced my own. Even if it is only for a brief while."

"That can never happen," Mother snapped. "Do you understand? We are not like them. We are what keeps them safe for their pitifully short time alive."

Maiden sulked, "All beings die eventually. We too shall join them."

"We are different." Mother pulled out a snow-colored shawl and wrapped it around her broad shoulders. "When our cycle ends, we will elevate to a higher purpose. No one will pass judgment or decide our eternity for us."

"But—"

"Enough, Maiden." Mother closed the mirrored doors. "You must not spend your time creating stories about mortals. Tartarus is in need of our full attention."

"You and Crone discuss our home like it is living. It is only chambers and halls like the other levels of the Underworld." Maiden studied her reflection in the wardrobe and improved her slumping posture.

"Do you think it is our beauty that protects the mortals and keeps the evils of this world locked away?"

Maiden twirled the ends of her long auburn hair and shrugged. "I suppose not."

"Think, for a moment, on the true evil we jail."

"What of it?"

Mother sighed and sat next to Maiden on the bed. "If even one of those creatures freed itself and traveled up, how would we protect ourselves from their vengeance? How would we protect the mortals you care so deeply for? We must respect our home. It is alive around us, protecting both ourselves and the Mortal Realm from destruction."

Maiden ran her fingers over the crystal amulet hanging around her neck. "But that is not possible. Nothing can escape from Tartarus."

"It is only impossible until it is not."

Maiden's forehead wrinkled. "I do not understand."

"Sister, anything is possible. If the wickedness within this prison made it to the Mortal Realm, we would be destroyed and hell would reign on earth. All the good you see in the human race would wither without Tartarus."

"I still do not see the need to classify the mortals so hastily."

Mother sighed. "Sometimes I wonder if you will ever learn." She patted Maiden on the leg. "I may not be able to teach you our history and purpose in one day, but I can open your eyes to some truth. Come with me."

Maiden hopped off the bed and followed Mother down a brightly lit hallway. The floor and walls gleamed a glassy white, and Maiden admired her distorted reflection all the way down the narrow passageway.

Mother stopped abruptly, and Maiden crashed into her back.

"Apologies." She giggled.

The stern look on her sister's face made her smile fade.

"Final Judgment takes place just beyond that gate."

She followed Mother's gaze. Tartarus's foreboding entry gate cast thick shadows on the floor. "I thought I was not to watch Final Judgment."

"You need to see what I know to be true. Mortals plead for either eternal freedom in Elysium or mercy in condemnation. Watch the next Final Judgment. See for yourself what simple creatures mortals are. Maybe then you will stop creating stories." Mother brushed past her sister and disappeared down the hall.

Maiden crossed her arms and lowered her green eyes to the crisscrossed pattern of shadows. "There is nothing wrong in thinking there is more to them. Besides, are not all stories based in truths?" Maiden said, sliding her bare feet across the smooth floor.

The narrow hall felt smaller as she approached the grand gate. The stench of decay wafted from the Acheron River, and Maiden covered her nose to keep from gagging.

"Charon, bring us the next soul for Final Judgment," a voice thundered from one of the three high-backed platinum chairs at the mouth of the Acheron.

Although their seats hid the figures, she recognized the voice. "Aeacus," she whispered, quickening her pace. She reached the gate and stood on her tiptoes to see over its filigree designs.

Charon's skiff drunkenly bobbed along the waters of the Acheron. Its lone passenger held his arms out to steady himself as Charon guided the boat to shore.

"Your time has come." Charon's bony arm pointed

to the chairs. "Go, face your judgment, but do not forget to leave my payment." His long beard seemed to pull him down; a small hump formed between his shoulder blades.

The soul stood and dropped his fare by Charon's feet. It hit the vessel with a hollow thud. "Your coin, Charon," he said, bowing low before he disembarked.

"Galen Argyris, your life in the Mortal Realm has ended. Your soul now faces Final Judgment. Only two choices remain, Elysium or the Underworld. How do you believe your soul has been colored?" Aeacus thundered.

"I am innocent." He stood tall before the panel, too proud to bend to the river's stench. "But I am not deserving of a place in Elysium. I made a deal in the Mortal Realm to trade my soul for that of my son."

"You wish to relinquish your soul's right to Elysium to spare your son?" A second voice reverberated through the chamber.

"I do, Rhadamanthus. The seer assured me the pact we made would be accepted," Galen said.

"And it will, unless you change your fate. The agreement you reached in the Mortal Realm can be quickly overturned," Aeacus said.

Rhadamanthus leaned forward. "Your son lit fire to a villa, causing the death of four mortals. Condemnation for taking life is severe. It will feel even more so as it has been earned by another."

"Those lives were not taken on purpose." Sorrow touched Galen's voice. "My son deserves a second chance. I will not go back on my word. I accept whatever may come with the fate I have chosen."

Maiden's calves ached, and she squeezed the gate's

swirling bars to steady herself.

"Galen Argyris, the Underworld will be your home. You will be trapped for eternity within its gates, and it will drain you of all happiness and hope. Do you understand?" the third voice boomed.

Galen nodded. "Yes, Minos."

Minos continued, "Your fate has been decided. Enter Tartarus and await your warden. You cannot escape or change this judgment. It is final and binding."

The gate vibrated and Maiden ducked into the shadows. It clattered open and Galen's footsteps brought him closer to her. His shoulders slumped slightly as he walked past her, and Maiden couldn't resist the urge to call out to him.

"Galen!" Startled, he turned and Maiden stepped into the light. "Why did you do such a thing?" she blurted out.

Shock painted his face. "I did not imagine someone so beautiful would not be pure enough to enter Elysium."

Maiden blushed. "You think I am beautiful?"

"More than any creature in the Mortal Realm."

"But I am not of your realm. I am Maiden, sister to Mother and Crone."

"You are one of the Furies?" Embarrassment seeped into his voice, and he bowed respectfully. "My apologies. I was taken aback by your presence. It is an honor to be in your company."

She stepped closer to him and placed her hand on his back. "Please, do not apologize. I am the one who is honored."

His bright gray eyes reflected the shimmering light of Tartarus. "There is no reason you have to feel honored. I am awaiting condemnation."

"I watched and know what occurred." She clasped her hands in front of her. "I wish my sisters could have also seen your judgment."

He smiled and shook his head. "I don't know that I would have been as brave with all three Furies as witnesses."

"I am certain nothing would have changed your mind. However, seeing you would have strengthened my argument and proven their belief erroneous."

"What belief is that?"

"They think there are only two paths mortals choose while in the Mortal Realm. The path of good, which leads to Elysium, or that of damnation, which has its beginnings here. For them, there is no other route."

Galen shook his head. "There are always other paths. We are faced with their challenges daily."

"That is something I have known in my heart to be true, but have never been able to convince my sisters. But the path you chose must have been one of good to earn you entry to Elysium."

"By the laws of the Underworld, I did nothing to prevent my access into Elysium, but I did not lead an admirable life." Galen's smile melted and his stare lowered. "I was not a good father. My son made many mistakes because of my failings."

"Of what failings do you speak?"

"I was a merchant, and traveled many miles trading goods to give my son the monies needed to lead a comfortable life."

"I hear nothing deserving of the fate you sought out," Maiden said.

"In truth, I was selfish." The light in his eyes dimmed as sorrow took hold. "After my wife passed into Elysium, I did not need to be away from my son. I only did so to drown myself in the comfort of women and forget my own pain. I never thought of my son's pain, and I did not prove myself as the strong father he needed."

She held his hand and squeezed it gently. "You did prove yourself. In the choice you made here. You could be free in Elysium, but instead you saved that gift for him. There is nothing you could have done that would be more important than that decision."

"I could have taught him how to be a man of honor. He deserves the eternal happiness I did not provide him during my time with the living."

"Galen Argyris." A cloaked figure stood at the mouth of the hall. "It is time. Follow me."

"Thank you, Maiden." He pressed his warm lips against the back of her hand. "I did not know such joy and light could exist in the Underworld."

Maiden held her hand against her chest, and sadness crept into her as Galen walked to his fate.

Weeks passed, and Maiden's heart ached with thoughts of Galen's suffering. So much so that she often snuck into the level where he served his condemnation. She soothed her heartsickness and provided him the joy he lacked.

"I am dreading the day I do not see you again," he said, his attention fixed on the picturesque villa before them. Smoke swirled around the estate and fire lapped against its outer walls.

"I cannot stay away from you, nor do I want to," she said warmly as she snuggled up to him.

He blindly searched for her hand and squeezed it gently.

"Let us not spend our time together here. Come with me." She tugged at his arm, but he didn't budge.

"I cannot," he said flatly.

"Do you grow tired of me? Look at me, Galen," she pleaded.

He strained to turn his face to hers.

"I…I do not understand," she stammered.

"This is the soul imprint of the events that lead to my son's damnation. Every day I build this home, and every night I'm powerless, forced to watch the family burn."

She cupped his face and turned his head back to the fire. "Do not struggle against your condemnation. I do not wish to cause you pain."

"Maiden, you are worth enduring the pain." The fire blazed in his soft, gray eyes. "You bring Elysium with you and make this eternity bearable."

She leaned into him and kissed him slowly. Neither of them breathed as the fire raged behind her.

• • •

Maiden's forbidden romance ensued with the innocent soul who traded his place in Elysium.

True love, this clean emotion, was a virgin to Tartarus. Its light never before touched so deep within the Underworld. Because of this light, this love borne in the condemned depths of the twinkling ice cave of Tartarus, a curse formed. It breathed toxins into the glassy cave walls, creating viscous strings that hung thick and wet. They dripped into its once serene turquoise pools turning them into acidic, milky mazes that coursed through Tartarus's veins.

The infected level could no longer contain its prisoners, and they tore free. Powerless against the waves of evil beings escaping to claim the mortal world as their own, the Furies watched helplessly as the freed inmates spewed venom throughout humanity. Corruption, plague, and brutality swept the Mortal Realm.

Desperate, Maiden beseeched Hera, Goddess of childbirth, asking her to come to their aid and heal the ailing Tartarus. Hera took pity on Maiden and gifted her with a child, created from the passion of her forbidden love. "You will birth a son," Hera whispered into Maiden's ear. "Your son will grow to be a warrior, tasked only to slay the wicked who escaped to the Mortal Realm and send them back to the prison within Tartarus. As he restores the balance, the curse will wane."

When Maiden first held her baby boy, she felt apprehension rather than joy. "He cannot leave," she cried, calling upon Hera once more.

"And he shall not," Hera replied. "He must stay in the Underworld, for that is where he draws his strength. Being exposed for too long in the mortal world will weaken him and steal his divine gifts."

Maiden gazed lovingly at the tiny bundle in her arms, her beautiful boy. "My warrior child. How am I to raise him for this task?"

Her sisters appeared, gently taking the child from her arms. While Crone laid the child in his bassinet to let Maiden rest, Mother soothed her troubled spirit. "You shall not do it alone, sister. We shall have help."

ONE

Twenty-Three Years Later

"Do you think he is ready?" Maiden's worry reverberated off of the barren cave walls. Their luster had faded long ago, replaced by a lifeless chalky gray.

"He has spent enough days training in the Mortal Realm. It is time he proves himself worthy of the title of warrior." Mother turned the corner to the innermost chamber. Her sisters hustled to keep up with her rushed pace as the once smooth floors flaked under their feet.

"I do not want to see him hurt because he has not been well enough prepared," Maiden whined.

"The last of the pools in the Hall of Echoes has begun to dry up, and with it our ability to see our enemies in the Mortal Realm. There is no way of knowing when they will overtake the mortals and if they are gathering together to destroy us. He must be prepared, and now," Mother said.

Maiden pleaded, "He has only been tested against lowly tricksters. You know they are nothing in comparison to the great evil that escaped from our walls. They did not even have an effect on the curse when he sent their bodies down to us."

Crone paused and laid a bony hand on Maiden's arm. She caught her breath and said, "Mother is correct. Our son is our only remaining defense, and we cannot wait any longer. The fate of more than just Tartarus is at stake."

"I understand." Maiden was silenced, but only momentarily. "But if they are plotting against us, it will do no good to thrust an unprepared boy in their path."

"Boy?" Mother stopped at the entry to the large dark chamber. Frustration controlled her voice, and she shouted back her retort. "Your judgment is clouded. You cannot see him for what he is. He is a young man."

"Sisters!" Crone hissed. "This is not the time to bicker. We must have faith in our teachings and in our son. When we summon him, there will be no more talk of doubts." Her blue eyes lingered on Maiden.

Mother's hand slid to her hip. "Then you believe he will succeed, wise sister?"

"I do not pretend to know what his future holds," Crone said and proceeded into the chamber.

"I suppose now our only hope is to trust in him and everything he has learned during his time in the Mortal Realm," Maiden said, following her eldest sister into the hollow space.

"Like Tartarus, this plan is cursed," Mother muttered.

"Enough!" Crone's voice surrounded the women. "He will never succeed while you are in possession of such negative thoughts. This discussion ends now. We have no choice. No more time can be spent debating. Tartarus will not bow to the evil it once jailed, and the Mortal Realm will not fall to its wickedness. We must act now. Come together, sisters."

Maiden, Mother, and Crone joined hands and spoke as one. "Alek, we summon thee." From their cave twisted deep within the Underworld, the Furies, daughters of night, beckoned their son home.

Swirls of brilliant energy spun together as Alek appeared. The air around him shimmered in waves from the heat of his skin. The trip home stunned him for only a moment. He straightened to his full height, tucked a blond curl behind his ear, and opened his arms, flashing a gallant smile. "It is good to see you, Mothers!"

"And you, Alek." Maiden pulled him close, enveloping him in the refreshing scents of honey and citrus as her head pressed into his chest. "It is wonderful that you are home and safe. It seems an eternity since you last were here."

"It has only been a matter of days," Alek protested.

"We know, Son. Time ticks by slowly below." Crone spoke softly. Her smooth silver hair glistened in the lifeless tomb their home had become.

"True, but the days are too long," Alek said, rolling his neck and stretching his thick shoulder muscles. "I feel like shit. I am weak and achy and tired."

Crone caressed his cheek. Her savory smells of sage and wet earth washed over him, soothing his restless body. "We are...pleased...that your speech has adapted so well to the Mortal Realm. Well enough to blend as one of them, but you must not forget that your home is a different land." She gave his cheek a light slap. "Watch your tongue while you are in the presence of your mothers."

He sighed deeply.

Mother squeezed his hand before ushering him farther into the poorly lit cavern. "Your training, how has it progressed?"

Her cinnamon and vanilla scents fought for attention, and he stifled a sneeze. Her scent was the most powerful, but it bordered on overwhelming. "You have brought me back from Vologda. It is in deepest Russia where the cold is intense and the winds are so strong they can cut a man in half." Alek looked to Maiden's eyebrows, arched in worry. He loved spinning his tales of heroism for his youngest mother. "Though my mission was extremely dangerous, I managed to pursue and trap Solomon, the escaped soul. You should find him back where he belongs," he added smugly.

Mother rolled her eyes. "Solomon was a thief. He stole medicine from his village and sold it."

"A dangerous thief," Alek muttered, his pride wounded.

"Son, I have seen Solomon. He was as round as he was tall in death, just as he was in life. I have no doubt you did well and that your training has prepared you, but you have greater foes to encounter."

"I have yet to meet an opponent I did not crush."

"You have only been to the Mortal Realm but a handful of times, and have yet to meet a *worthy* opponent."

"I assure you, Mother, when I do, the outcome will be no different. I haven't trained long, but I *will* prove myself as the Immortal Warrior of Tartarus, and our home shall finally be rid of this curse."

"You would run headfirst into a brick wall so long as you

leave an Alek-shaped hole in it afterward," Crone chuckled.

Maiden swept her auburn hair off her shoulders as she took a seat at the granite table. "That is why we have called you home, my son. The last looking pool in the Hall of Echoes has grown dark. We can no longer see into the Mortal Realm."

"We are defenseless," Mother added gravely.

"You are not defenseless. You have me, Mothers. Send me back to the Mortal Realm, and I will be your eyes." He pulled out a chair and sat next to Maiden.

"And we shall. However, it is true that you have not been training long, and this matter must not be mishandled. The price is too great," Crone said.

"I know what's at risk; the lives of mortals and our place in the Underworld. I will succeed."

"This is not a battle that can be fought and won in one day. It took centuries to capture the evil chained in this realm. You would be a fool to think you could do the same so quickly," said Mother.

"I am not a fool, and I cannot be afraid to act. The evil loosed in the Mortal Realm must learn to fear me as they once feared the great Tartarus," Alek said sternly.

"With time, they will, my son." Maiden placed a hand on his shoulder. "And with help, you will bring about change much more quickly than you could alone. The spirit of Pythia bestowed upon us an amazing gift with which to aid you."

Crone sat herself next to Mother. "She has gifted us each with a piece to locate one of her descendants so you might resurrect the ancient Oracle strength still living in her bloodline. As you are only too aware, you are able to walk in the mortal world, but if you venture there too long you will lose your immortality and other divine gifts. You cannot save the mortals if their world has drained you of all that is required to help them. Together, you and this descendant of Pythia will bring about the end of Tartarus's darkness and free the Mortal Realm of ancient evil."

"I do not need help, Mothers," Alek insisted. "Whoever he is, he will only get in my way."

"No," Crone corrected gently. "*He* will not. And *he* is not a *he*."

"The person who is to fight beside me as my equal is a girl?" He crinkled his brow. "I have been around girls, Mothers. I have seen how they act in the Mortal Realm. They are not like any of you. How is a *girl* supposed to help me protect and restore Tartarus and the Mortal Realm?"

"And that is all he heard." Crone drew in a deep breath from her place at the head of the table. "Your appearance will stay youthful forever, but it is my hope that that is the only part of you that does so." The ladies' laughter made the air around them twinkle and the moonflowers in the center of the table burst suddenly into blooms the delicate color of infants' flesh.

"She is not simply a *girl*," Mother corrected. "She is a descendant of Pythia."

"And who is Pythia?"

"You will learn. Call upon her. She has foreseen this and will come," Maiden assured.

"If she has foreseen this, why does she not come now? Why must I summon her?"

"Respect." Crone's glare bored into him. "Pythia is the first Oracle of Delphi. She will not assist if the proper channels are not followed."

"Then I better get started. If she's waiting for me to call, it shouldn't be too difficult." Alek closed his eyes and tried to speak in his most powerful voice. "Pythia—no. No, let me start over." He cleared his throat. "Pythia, come to me." He could feel the women rustle in annoyance as nothing happened. "Oracle, I call upon you." Alek cracked his eyes opened and was met with the faces of three discontented mothers. "She's not listening."

"Alek!" The Furies' voices melded together as they reprimanded their son. "You are a warrior of the Underworld. The ability to call upon the Oracle, or any God, lives within you. Focus!"

He immediately straightened and did as his mothers commanded. Alek focused, searching inside himself to harness the Grecian blood fueling his abilities. Again he closed his eyes. "Pythia!" A commanding voice he almost didn't recognize as his own surged from him. "Ancient Oracle, show yourself! I seek guidance. Let me learn from you my future."

A woman's breathy laughter filled his ears. Eagerly, he opened his eyes. A beaming white figure materialized and danced behind his mothers as it came into focus.

The Furies stood, turned, and bowed before the specter. "Welcome to Tartarus, Oracle of Delphi."

"I accept your invitation. Sit."

"The invitation was not ours, Oracle." Maiden gestured to Alek as Pythia noticed the young man and turned a curious gaze to him.

"Pythia, I'm glad you could come." Alek's eyes roamed across her body. She was gorgeous, with eyes like amber gems pressed into a perfect sculpture. A thick fall of moonlight-

21

colored hair rested on bare breasts while her see-through skirts played around her legs.

"Hm. He looks human. Tastes..." A tongue snaked from her mouth and writhed in the air, "human. Even sounds human. But, what is it?"

"I'd be happy to let you inspect me further. After dinner in the Mortal Realm, perhaps?" He smirked.

The corners of her mouth lifted. "Come here."

As Alek's strides brought him closer to the ancient being, the heat from her skin became palpable.

"Closer." Pythia slowly bit her bottom lip as her jeweled gaze studied him intently. "You believe you could fulfill the desires of a powerful Oracle?"

"Of course." He grinned.

As Pythia's vision shifted, Alek watched her appearance do the same. For an instant, he no longer saw a goddess-like creature. Instead, her smile slashed her face from ear to ear releasing putrid tongues that flopped wet and limp like bloated, drowned fingers from their toothy den. Her eyes shuddered in their sockets, exhausted from centuries of glimpsing the future.

Alek forced himself not to cringe away from her.

"You could not conceive of how to even begin to satisfy me. Perhaps you should focus your," her brows lifted sardonically, "*talents* on young mortals. I seem to remember they are more easily amused." More laughter spilled from her lips and playfully twirled through his hair, making the skin on the back of his neck tingle.

Alek felt redness build in his cheeks, and he retreated to his mothers' side. "You're not what I expected."

"Rarely is a woman," she purred. "Did you call upon me

because you are in need of guidance, or did you simply want a glimpse of something deliciously, irresistibly unattainable?"

Alek glanced at his mothers who nodded encouragement. He cleared his throat. "I summoned you because I need your help in finding one of your descendants."

"Really? *My* descendant? Why?" Her laughter was seductively sarcastic.

"She is to assist me in my mission, although I'm not sure what role a girl will play in battle."

Light ripped through the black hall as Pythia screeched. Her curvy figure rocketed to twice its normal size, engorged with power.

"There is much you do not understand. Questions penned on your face and through your being. Hollow as ice. You sample from the plate of a world and a time of which you know nothing and wonder why it is so bitter." She glowed hot gold as her voice hardened. "I am the Oracle of Delphi. My prophecies halted war and ravaged men. Power so great and awarded by the Gods is not easily diluted. A mortal *girl* carries this magic within her blood, within her bones. I can hear it sighing, sleeping in her lungs and her blood until it is awakened." The vibrant figure's colors cooled, and her body contracted. "Until *you* awaken it."

Realizing he was very close to cowering behind a chair, Alek squared his shoulders and his will; he stepped forward, and in a voice that almost didn't crack, said, "How?"

"Only at the moment when her mortal heart ceases to beat will her destiny ignite and the strengths of the Oracle become free. This will be the future, or your beloved Tartarus will decay beyond repair, and you will be responsible for its extinction." Pythia's gaze held Alek's as she faded into

23

nothing. A roar of laughter echoed in her absence.

Confused, Alek collapsed back into his chair.

"The Fates have decided. The young woman's cord of life is being cut," Maiden said, covering his hand with hers.

"Her mortal existence will end," Mother explained, cupping his free hand.

"However, you will be there to intercept and rewrite her future," Crone said, looking to her sisters. She took their hands, closing the circle.

Alek remained still, stunned, and uncertain. He watched as each of his mothers settled, and with a combined hum, they opened their eyes and mouths in unison. From their eyes poured an amber smoke. It swirled into Alek's nose and filled his chest. He writhed in his chair. The Furies held his hands tighter, pinning him to the stone table with strength only found in immortals.

In unison their luminous lips formed words that hit Alek's ears with a boom. "We have breathed into you a piece of each of us, which you must give to the heir of Pythia. Fill her with these fractured pieces of our souls so they may become whole and return life to the lifeless."

The Furies deflated and flopped back in their chairs like cast-off marionettes. Overwhelmed by the power crackling within his chest, branded to his lungs, Alek struggled to suck in air and get to his feet. The smoky souls that infiltrated his body were too much. He groped the air for anything to steady his shuddering body. Finding nothing and unable to call out, he crumpled to the floor and surrendered to the soft blackness overwhelming his vision.

TWO

"Eva, stop messing with it and turn around," Lori said impatiently.

Eva dropped her hands to her sides and stared at her reflection in the mirror. The top hugged her slender waist, accentuating the curve of her hourglass figure. "It fits great in some places, but not so great in others. I really want this to work, though. I have the perfect skirt to go with it, and it would look great at the party." She gave it one last tug before turning around to face her mother.

Lori scrunched her nose. "You look like you're about to audition for a beer commercial."

Eva let out a sigh and turned back to the mirror. "It's because I have these giant boobs." She tried unsuccessfully to stuff her cleavage into the shirt.

"It's our family curse. Luckily, after you have kids someday in the future, the very distant future, you can do what I did and have them reduced."

"Like I'll ever have time to have kids. School is already

killing me, and the semester just started. Plus, it's Bridget's mission to fill up my social calendar and make sure we're on the board of every nonprofit that will take twenty-three-year-old members. And to make matters even worse, I'm busy beating off every ridiculous boy-man who thinks I'm on the seven-year college plan just to get a husband."

Lori chuckled. "You're going to get carpal tunnel."

Eva's cheeks reddened. "That is not what I meant at all. I mean, like, literally beating them back. But not literally. I haven't hit anyone, yet." She leaned closer to the mirror and picked away a few clumps of mascara.

"I was lucky and met your dad in college. Don't discount any of those boy-men just yet."

Even though it had been just the two of them for the past decade, talking about her dad still made Eva uncomfortable. "So this top is a no?"

"A definite no. Why don't you try that pretty green dress?" Lori pointed to the rack of clothes. "It'll look really good with your skin tone."

Eva peeled off the snug top and walked across the large dressing room. "This one?" She slipped the dress off the hanger and held it out in front of herself.

"It is going to look great. A lot better than trying to squeeze yourself into clothes that are too small. It'll outline your curves without throwing them in someone's face. You don't want people to say hi to your boobs before they even notice the rest of you."

"I guess. I just want to look as old as I am, instead of getting carded for movies."

"In ten years you'll wish you were still getting carded."

Eva centered herself in front of the mirror. "But this is

a party. I don't want to look like I'm going to church."

"You don't want to look like a big ol' ho bag either. Just try it on. I think you'll be surprised." Lori crossed her legs and leaned back in her chair.

Eva threw her long brunette hair to the side as she stepped into the dress.

"Who all is going to this party?" Lori asked.

"A few girls I hang out with sometimes, and Bridget, of course. Other than that, I'm not really sure," she said, wiggling the dress up her body.

"What about any guys you're interested in? I know that you're busy, but there has to be someone you have your eye on."

"There might be, but I don't want to talk about it." She guided the soft straps over her shoulders.

"Why not?"

"Because, Mom," Eva said with a sigh. "It always turns into some kind of awkward safe sex talk."

"I just want to make sure you're protected and know you can talk to me about anything."

"I understand, but I'm an adult. You don't have to worry about guys and me anymore. I've got it handled. I promise." Eva smiled at her mom's reflection. "Now for the moment of truth." She awkwardly stretched her arm around her back to reach the zipper.

Lori gasped. "It's stunning, Eva."

"You were totally right." The soft chiffon tickled her thighs as she twirled in front of the dressing room mirror. "And the high neckline looks amazing." She stood on her tiptoes to better envision what she would look like in heels. "Way less churchy than I thought it would be."

"See? I know fashion. Now, let's go find some shoes."

Eva sucked in an excited gulp of air. "Shoes?!"

Lori collected her purse and opened the dressing room door. "For me, not you. Come find me after you're dressed."

Eva exhaled and slowly changed back into her clothes. "Good thing we wear the same size shoes."

She hung the dress back on its hanger and draped it over her arm. She took one more look at herself and smoothed out her frizzy flyaways before leaving the dressing room.

"Mom?" Eva stretched out her neck and called out over the racks of clothing. "Lori?"

"Over here!" Eva spotted her mother's arms flailing next to the end of season shoe sale rack.

"Coming!" she called back.

"What do you think about these?" Lori opened the shoebox once Eva was in range. Nestled among white tissue paper lay a pair of sparkly gold wedges.

"Super cute!" Eva chirped. "Are they on sale?"

Lori scoffed. "Of course not. They're Jimmy Choos."

"I thought we were only getting stuff that's on sale."

"No, *you're* only getting stuff that's on sale because you don't have a job. I, however, can get what I want." She grinned.

"But you told me that my job is finishing school." Eva followed her mom to the store's purse section.

"Right."

"Okay, but that doesn't make any sense. I can't buy my own stuff because I don't have a job because you told me not to get one."

"Right." Lori held up a designer handbag and looked at herself in the mirror. The round mound of frizzy multicolored tassels reminded Eva of something she pulled out of their clogged vacuum.

Eva scrunched her nose. "I wouldn't go with that one." Lori hung it back on the rack. "So, I'm totally confused, and I feel like I'm being punished for still being in school." Eva pooched out her bottom lip.

"You know damn well you're not being punished. And you're twenty-three years old. That pouty face you have on doesn't work on me anymore."

She shrugged. "It was worth a try."

Lori pulled another purse from the rack and modeled it in front of the mirror.

"It's been a while since you've said anything about William." Eva demonstrated her best Downton Abbey accent when pronouncing his name. "Well, not since he left for Mexico. Is he back yet?"

"Bill's been back for a while now. Remember, we saw him a couple weeks ago when we were at Home Depot getting more birdseed?"

Eva looked blankly at her mom while she searched her memories.

Lori continued, "He was buying those chains to help the guys who are renovating his basement."

Eva had met Bill only once before, but something about the way he looked at her that day had made her skin crawl. He hadn't been inappropriate, and Eva couldn't even pinpoint what made her so uncomfortable. There was just something off about him. *I'm sure it's something that you've made up in your head. Don't go all crazy, possessive daughter because your mom finally has a boyfriend.* She forced the images from her mind.

"Well, I've seen him a couple times since the store,

but…" Lori trailed off.

"You're going to fire him, aren't you? Oh my God, he's totally fired," Eva blurted, surprised by how much joy the thought brought her.

"No, he's not going anywhere. I still like him. I know you've only seen him a couple times, but you like him, right?"

Eva looked away from her mom and shrugged. "I don't really know him."

Lori's shoulders slumped slightly, and she hung the bag back on the rack.

"But, when I did meet him, he seemed really great," she lied, instantly regretting not supporting her mom. "And from everything you've told me, he's really nice too."

"True, but he's been kind of different ever since he came back from that mission trip. You'd think setting out on a road trip to go help people build houses would make him more appreciative, not weird." The mall was busy with Labor Day sales shoppers, and Lori led the way to the long line for the register. "I'm not really sure how to explain it, I guess." She adjusted the shoebox she held on her hip like a baby.

"Now I'm invested in the story. You have to try to explain. You can't just stop there. How is he being different? I need specifics." Eva took a moment to think about what she'd said then added, "But not too specific, of course."

"Well, he's not as affectionate and gentlemanly as he was before. He used to hold my hand, open doors for me, rub my feet. He hasn't done any of that since he's been home."

"I wouldn't want to rub your feet either." Eva chuckled and pinched the tip of her nose.

"I'm being serious, Eva."

"Okay, okay. Sorry. He might be scared. Didn't you tell

me that you're the first person he's dated since his divorce? Maybe it's too soon for him." The line moved forward, and they shuffled closer to the checkout counter.

"Yeah, I guess he might feel like things have been moving too fast."

"You should talk to him tonight when you go out." She could tell her mom was upset and tried to brighten the mood. "Where are you guys going?"

"To the Lorton Performance Center at the university. I got free tickets from work to go see the ballet perform tonight. I know you hate any stage performance that doesn't involve singing, so Bill's going to be my date," Lori said, sounding a little more chipper.

"I don't hate the ballet. I just don't understand why they can't break out into song every once and a while. Life would just be so much better as a musical. When is Bill coming by to pick you up?"

"I'm taking my car, but he'll stop by the house for a second first. He's going to follow me to the Performance Center. We'll leave his car there if we go anywhere after."

"You still have an issue with the way he drives?"

"God, it's so annoying. He does the speed up, slow down, speed up, slow down thing. It makes me want to scream every time I'm in the car with him. But I think I've done a pretty good job avoiding the issue. Hence, the whole he's following me and we'll drop his car off when we need to thing. I really don't think he suspects anything."

"Yet," Eva interjected. "You can't refuse to ride with him forever."

"Sure I can. You never drive when we're together."

"You've been tricking me for the past seven years?

That's not very nice." They finally reached the register, and Eva carefully lowered the dress onto the counter.

"But you didn't figure it out until just now."

Eva opened her mouth but couldn't think of a witty retort. "True."

"Did y'all find everything okay today?" the cashier asked cheerily.

"Yes, thank you," Lori replied while digging through her luggage-size purse.

"Too bad you didn't find a smaller bag," Eva snickered.

"My purse works just fine, thank you. Everything I need is in here."

"Yeah, but you can't ever find exactly what you're looking for."

"Can too." Lori pulled out her wallet.

"Gross, Lori. It's covered in old Kleenex fuzz."

Lori put the tissue back in her purse. "But you love me anyway."

"Well, of course I love you. I just don't love all the dried up snot you carry with you."

Lori laughed and handed the cashier her credit card before she had time to announce the total.

"Thanks for the dress, Mom." Eva leaned the side of her head against her mom's. "I can't wait to wear it tonight."

"You're going to look beautiful. Just like your mama."

She and Lori linked arms and headed for the doors leading to the parking lot.

THREE

Mahna mahna. Do doo be-do-do. Mahna Mahna. Do do-do do.
Mahna Mahna. Do doo be-do-do be-do-do be-do-do be-do-do-
doddle do do do-doo do!

The Muppets alarm cheerfully squawked through Eva's
gold phone, waking her from a much-needed nap. She
groped around her bedside table for her bottle-cap lens
glasses, but instead knocked everything off to the floor.

"Shit!" She rolled to her side and felt around the carpet
for her glasses. "There you are." She used the bottom of her
shirt to wipe off the fingerprints before pushing them onto
her face.

She hung her head over the edge of the bed and picked
up the candle and picture frame she had pushed onto
the floor.

In the photo, a ten-year-old Eva flashed a wide smile at
the camera. Her arm stretched around an equally excited girl
with bright green eyes and messy blond pigtails.

Eva's ringtone blared, and she slid her thumb up the

face of the phone. "Hey! I was just thinking about you."

"I *am* all sorts of fabulous," Bridget replied.

"Do you remember when we got lost together in the rain forest exhibit at the zoo?" She flipped onto her back and held the picture above her face.

"Of course! And that weird bird wouldn't stop screeching and pulling my hair. He was doing me a favor though. I did look like that blond Powerpuff Girl. So embarrassing."

Eva snorted with laughter.

"But, that's the day we became best friends!" Bridget trilled. "We spent so much time there and at Mohawk Park. We definitely deserve some kind of plaque."

"For sure, and I think being attacked by a bird was worth it." Eva grinned, returning the picture to the table.

"So, what have you been doing since you got home from the mall?"

"Studying," she groaned.

"Studying?" Bridget enunciated the word like it was foreign. "I still can't figure out why you won't just hurry up and graduate."

"I can't decide on a major that I'll be good at and will actually land me a job when I get out of school. So I keep advancing, just to fall back when I switch. Not all of us can be as lucky as you are."

"Just because I have a trust fund doesn't mean I don't have a job," Bridget said, pretending to sound offended.

"You work twice a week at the cutest, most expensive clothing store in Tulsa."

"Right! That's sort of why I'm calling. I need to know what you're wearing tonight. I went by work earlier and picked up a few things, but I don't want to be so overdressed that it looks weird. But if you're going to be, like, super dressed up, then I'll get super dressed up, and we'll be super dressed up and gorgeous together!"

"Don't get too excited. I'm only going to be sort of dressed up. I'm wearing the new dress my mom bought me and her new gold shoes."

Bridget sucked in air. "The Jimmy Choos you texted me about? They're out of stock in my size, and I would kill to get my hands on those shoes. How did you get her to agree to that?"

Eva lay back on her bed. "I didn't. I just took them from her closet. But I'll put them back as soon as I get home, and she'll never even know they were gone. It's not like anything's going to happen to them."

"I wish I could borrow my mom's shoes. She has the most fabulous collection of Manolo's. But she also has huge Sasquatch feet, which totally ruins everything. Shit, hang on." Bridget moved the phone and only muffled whines seeped through to Eva. "Okay. Yes. I'm telling her right now. My mother says hi."

"Tell her I said hi back. Wait, why are you at your parents' house?"

"They're going to some kind of benefit charity thing tonight, and I had to drop off a dress she ordered from the store. And now I'm mooching food. Oh, she also wants me to tell you to Google the KOTV news clip about the murderer guy."

"What murderer guy?"

"I don't know. I try not to watch the news. It depresses me."

Eva's pillow squished farther into the bed as she shook

her head at her carefree friend. "But aren't we supposed to know what's going on in the world? Especially in our own town?"

"So, you check out the video and tell me if there's anything worth knowing. Unless, of course, it's like gross or sad or something." Eva heard Bridget's please-and-thank-you smile through the phone. "And I have to get back to my condo and finish putting my face on. I'll see you tonight at the Ambassador!"

"Sounds good. I'll see you soon!"

Eva tapped the glowing "end" square on her phone.

"Eva! Do you know where my new wedges are?" Her mother's shouts grew louder as she closed in on Eva's room. "I just bought them, and they've already *mysteriously* disappeared."

Eva hefted herself off the bed and met Lori in the doorway. "Umm, nope. Haven't seen 'em."

"Damn. Bill's going to be here," she began as she brushed her thick brown hair behind her ear and glanced down at her watch, "in less than an hour, and I have no idea where they are."

"Maybe you accidently covered up the box with something." Eva felt the lie painting her cheeks red. She squeezed through the doorway and quickly walked to the stairs before Lori could notice.

"That does sound like me. They're probably sitting in plain sight somewhere. If you see them let me know," Lori called after her.

"Will do," Eva shouted. She tried to shake the icky-lie feeling from her shoulders as she headed for the refrigerator. "It's not like I was really lying. Just bending the truth." She grabbed hummus and a chopped cucumber from the fridge. "Okay, bending the truth is lying, but whatever. Tomorrow, it won't matter. She'll have her shoes back. No big deal."

She dunked a cucumber slice into the hummus and took a bite. The familiar flavors brought her back to being a little girl. She could practically smell the lamb cooking on the stovetop while her Yiayiá waddled around the kitchen, instructing Eva in broken English on the proper knife holding technique.

"Like this, Eva. Like this. Then slice. Now try, try." Yiayiá had placed a cucumber on a cutting board and put a sharp blade into Eva's hand, handle side first. Then she stood back and observed.

Eva had made one slice before her finger got in the way. The blood hadn't scared her, and now she couldn't even remember the pain, the only thing she could remember was her Yiayiá. The elderly woman wailed. "Oh no, no, no," she chanted, along with some choice phrases in Greek. She rushed to Eva, towel in hand, and pressed against the wound. "No cut no more. I cut," she insisted. "I cut." Yiayiá clutched Eva tight to her ample bosom, the scent of anisette and lamb powerful and intoxicating. After a few minutes rocking her back and forth, Yiayiá took the towel off of Eva's wound. "Good yes? Like new?" she examined the tiny cut on Eva's finger, now mostly clotted. Yiayiá took down a bandage and wrapped it. Eva proudly sported the sparkly bandage until it grew dingy and fell off in the tub. Eva remembered her Yiayiá returning to the lamb, but looking at the towel, at the small speckles of blood, and saying to herself, in perfect English, "I can see it. There, in her blood. Listen as it whispers to you. She must die to live again."

That sour turn of the memory made Eva's stomach clench. She put the food back in the fridge and jogged upstairs to her room.

Lori followed her in with a sigh. "I have no idea what I did with my shoes. I can't find them anywhere."

Eva walked to the radish-colored bathroom attached to her mauve bedroom. "Bummer. Sorry you can't find your shoes. Need a pair of mine?"

"No, I'm going to wear these. It's frustrating because I know they're here somewhere, but I don't have time to look. Bill's going to be early. Just wanted to let you know that I'm heading out."

Eva poked her finger into one eye, waiting for the familiar suction feel of the contact before leaning out of the doorframe to respond. "Have fun tonight."

"You too. And don't forget to call for an Uber if you drink. Or you can call me. I'm sure I'll be home early enough to be your designated."

"Will do."

"Eva?"

Eva looked up. "What's up?"

"Be responsible tonight."

"Always."

Lori turned to leave, but spun back around. "Eva?"

"What?"

"Also have fun. Be responsible but have fun. Ooooh, be responsible for having fun." Pleased with herself, Lori grabbed her keys and smiled.

Eva watched her mom slowly turn to leave, still scanning the floor for her sparkly shoes, and hoped she would age as gracefully. Lori's voluptuous frame was reminiscent of the great Marilyn Monroe, and the thin laugh lines that crept from the corners of her almond eyes gave a nod to her happy spirit. She was way too pretty for Bill, and Eva didn't understand what her mom saw in him. Sure, he was attractive in a bland, plastic way, had money, and took her to nice places, but there was something off about him. The memory of him at Home Depot again entered Eva's mind. He was too smiley. Like the Joker. And he smelled funny. Not like stinky garbage funny, or even old man funny, just *funny*. But Bill was the first man who'd made her mom happy since her dad left.

"Oh well," Eva sighed aloud to her reflection. She didn't care whether or not her mom dated, but she didn't like to think about her dad abandoning them. Eva studied herself in the mirror. It had been so long since she had seen her dad in person; she had a hard time identifying which parts of her face belonged to him. She had her mother's almond-shaped eyes, round face, high cheekbones, and full lips. It wasn't that she didn't know what her father looked like. Lori swooned and called Eva into the living room each time John Stamos came on TV advertising Greek yogurt. She swore Dean could be his doppelganger, and from the pictures Eva saw, she wasn't too far off. Thanks to John Stamos, and some very old photos, Eva knew her tan skin tone was because of her father. She brought her hand to her face. *Is this his nose?*

Rooooaaarrr! Chewbacca's howl went off, signifying a new text, and she fought the urge to squeal.

Bridget: My mom won't get out of my ass about sending you this. She can't work her new phone so here's the link. I'll let her know that you got it. I'm almost ready! See you very soon! Bring mace!

Eva clicked on the attached link and the messaging

screen promptly traded places with a YouTube app.

"Good evening, I'm Chera Kimiko. We begin with tonight's Green Country Crime Report. Talia Kirk is live outside the Tulsa County Sheriff's Office with more. Talia?"

A cute, bright-eyed young woman stood before the camera and, when prompted by Chera, began her well-scripted synopsis of events. "Chera, detectives are working hard tonight to find the person or persons responsible for a recent deadly attack. With the number of violent crimes in Tulsa rising, Chief of Police Gordon Charles had this to say: 'Our city is expanding at a high rate, but we are confident in our efforts to keep its citizens safe. If you have any information about this attack, or any other crimes, please call our sheriff's office anonymous tip line.' Back to you, Chera."

"Thank you, Talia. If you have any information that might help investigators, please call 596-COPS. Up next, ten tips to stay safe over the Labor Day holiday weekend."

The clip froze and went silent as a picture of downtown Tulsa appeared on screen. Eva set down the phone in exchange for a bronze eye shadow palette.

"Moral of the story, don't visit sketchy parts of town."

FOUR

"Gentlemen, my official medical opinion is that I haven't seen anything this fucked up in dog years." Medical Examiner Catherine Pierce greeted the detectives as they entered through the swinging double doors and into the morgue. Fluorescent lights buzzed from the outdated white ceiling tiles.

Detective Schilling's gruff Oklahoma twang coated his words. "What do we got here?" He rubbed a hand through his silvering temples before resting his arms on his thick abdomen.

"Ligature marks on the wrists and ankles. There's a band across her forehead like something was used to hold her head back. Hemorrhaging around the throat. Multiple stab wounds to the right arm, chest, abdomen, and legs. Most of them shallow, but some of them look deep." Pierce pointed at each part as she delivered her report. Detective Schilling grimaced as he studied the body. His partner, Detective James Graham forced his eyes to stay focused on the woman's pale corpse. Flecks of dark brown facial hair shimmered as James rhythmically clenched his jaw and circled the exposed, mutilated body. Pierce leaned closer. "Then there's this." She motioned to the left forearm, and Schilling and James both knelt to table height.

"Is that a tree?" James asked.

The black, leafless design looked like a shadow imprinted on white plastic. The trunk sprang from her wrist creases. Its intricate limbs gripped her toned arm and reached for her elbow.

James nodded. "The rest of the body is covered in gashes, except this arm. Whoever did this wants all our attention right here."

Pierce handed James the victim's file. "Schilling, it looks like the kid is a keeper."

Schilling grunted. "So the vic was bound, tattooed, tortured with a knife, and strangled."

"Not quite," Pierce said. "She wasn't alive when she was stabbed, but I can't say the same for the tattoo. It was done around two hours before death. Also, lividity on her shoulders, thighs, and torso points to her being on her back for some time before he moved her."

James opened the file and thumbed through it. "It says here the deceased was a chemical engineering student at the University of Tulsa with a full-ride track scholarship." He studied her colorless face. "Must've been smart. And fast too."

"Unfortunately, the suspect was faster." She disappeared behind Schilling's stocky frame and reappeared with a pair of latex gloves. She slipped them onto her slender hands and lifted the victim's arm. "She has defensive wounds on her hands and a few broken nails. I swabbed all of them, but I'm not too hopeful I'll get anything back. She was washed clean." Pierce lowered the arm and placed a gloved finger on the victim's forehead. Her vibrant red nail polish peeked through the latex, making the victim's skin appear even duller. "The markings you mentioned on her forehead, wrists, and ankles were made by the same type of device. Probably a belt or strap. You can tell by the extensive bruising that they were either very tight, or she struggled against them. My guess is he used them to keep her still while he tattooed her."

Schilling maintained his stoic posture and asked, "He, why do you think our suspect's a man?"

Pierce rolled her eyes. "It takes a strong set of hands to cause neck bruising like that." She stared down at the young woman. "It never gets any easier to look at, Detective Graham," she reminded.

James's gaze lingered on the victim's face. If he ignored his surroundings, she almost looked like she was sleeping. He blinked rapidly and turned his attention to the computer screen glaring down from above the body. A closeup image of the girl's left forearm seemed to be seared onto the screen.

He pointed at the image. "What do you think that is?"

"What do I think what is?" Schilling searched the screen for some kind of revelation.

James lowered his face to her forearm. "Hm." He stood up and looked at the screen, paused for a few moments, and then bent over her arm again.

"What is it?" Catherine asked, confused. "What do you see?"

"It's some type of scratch." James erected himself. "But it's a lot easier to see in the picture than it is on her. You guys don't see it?"

They each shook their head.

James spilled the file onto a nearby empty exam table. "That." He thrust a finger onto the hardcopy of the picture that appeared on the screen.

"Huh." Schilling picked up the photo and held it away from his aging eyes. The lines in his forehead deepened, his expression growing more puzzled. "Some sort of strange ridges on top of one of the tree limbs." He passed the picture to Pierce.

Her cheeks slowly turned pink. "Fuck me. Good eye, Graham. I'm pissed I missed it."

"You can make up for it by helping me get a better look at those ridges."

A smile tipped the corners of her mouth.

"We need to see this part of the tattoo." His finger floated over the victim's forearm, circling the area of interest.

Catherine rotated the arm so the palm was flat against the table. Gnarled branches continued on the back of the arm, and James examined them closely. "Now they're easier to see."

"Looks like they're supposed to be part of the tattoo." Schilling's sour coffee breath hit the back of James's neck as he spoke. "But you can't see any ink."

James lifted his gaze to meet Pierce's. "Do you have any idea what these marks are?"

Her short bob bounced as she shook her head. "To be honest, I was hoping you would know."

• • •

James drummed his fingers on his desk as he perused web pages for clues. They came back to the station after visiting the M.E.'s office to fill out some paperwork and so James could get his car. That had been three hours ago. Most of the officers and other detectives had cleared out. Only a few remained hunched over their keyboards sipping energy drinks while quietly mumbling to themselves. Finished for the night, Schilling sat at his desk across from James fidgeting impatiently. James tried unsuccessfully to ignore him.

"You don't have to wait for me," he said without taking his gaze off of the monitor. "But if you're going to sit there, you could always straighten up all of those piles. They look like they're about to topple over." The suggestion sounded harsher than he meant, but he didn't apologize.

Folders, fishing magazines, pale yellow Post-it notes, and newspapers from every day for the past two weeks covered Schilling's desk. In comparison to James's neatly organized and labeled workspace, it was a mess.

"You do know pretty much everything you have on there you can look at online?" James added.

Schilling eyeballed the heaps and grumbled. "Rookie cop mistake number seventy-three."

"I'm not a rookie," James said under his breath.

"Look Graham, sometimes you just got to know when to stop for the night. You need sleep. Hell, we both do. Cases like this aren't solved in one day, so there's no point in driving yourself crazy searching for needles in haystacks." Schilling stood and draped his jacket over his arm. "The body's not going anywhere. We'll find out more tomorrow."

"You ever see anything like that before?" he asked before Schilling started for the exit.

Schilling leaned against the back of his chair and thought for a moment. "I've seen a lot of things more brutal, but nothing so calculated."

"It's going to happen again, and it's probably happened before."

Schilling bristled. "Now don't rush to an assumption. You start doing that, and you're likely to twist all the evidence to support it. Rookie mistake number forty-one."

"It's specific and calculated, like you said. He practically left his signature on the body and washed away any other evidence. That kind of thing doesn't randomly happen one time. I guarantee it wasn't his first." James turned his attention back to the computer screen.

"I will say that he seems to have gone through a lot of trouble."

"Hey, I think I found something," James said.

"What is it?" Schilling tossed his coat on his desk and pulled out his chair. It squeaked and sank a few inches under his weight.

"At first I was focusing on the meaning behind the tree, but that led me nowhere. Nothing seemed to make any sense. So I changed gears and started researching tattoos. More specifically, the types of ink used."

"To explain the ridges found on the vic?" Schilling asked, wheeling his creaky chair next to James.

"Exactly." James rotated the monitor to accommodate his partner. "And I found a type of tattoo ink that's pretty much invisible in normal light, but when it's put under a UV light, it glows."

"Like those hand stamps they're giving people at clubs nowadays?"

James nodded. "Let's see if this clip has more info about it."

He made a few clicks of the mouse, and a close-up of a hand filled the screen. After a few seconds of silence, the camera panned out for a view of the man and the tattoo parlor he sat in. "Where I work, I can't have visible tattoos. So I choose to get UV ink tattoos done by Mike here at Tattoo Tavern. Getting UV ink tattoos is a way for me to express myself when I go out to clubs and bars, and not have people judge me when I'm at work or out in public with my kids."

As the camera zoomed back in on his hand, the tattoo artist took a seat opposite the customer. "You ready?"

The hand gave a thumbs up, and the room went black. "Check that out! My skeleton's almost done." On the hand, tattooed bones glowed a frosty white.

"All you'll have to do is carry a UV light around with you next Halloween, and you'll be set." The tattoo artist laughed. His gun whirred to life, and James hit pause.

"That has to be what our guy used on this victim."

Schilling put his hand on the edge of James's desk and hefted himself out of his chair. "There's only one way to find out."

"Right. I'll send Catherine a message and tell her we're coming by in the morning."

"And that we need one of those lights. Don't stay too late. I need you bright-eyed and bushy-tailed first thing," Schilling added, reaching to grab his jacket.

"I'll be ready," James said.

"Oh, and I'm also going to need you to come to dinner soon. Jeannine won't stop talking about meeting you. When you get a new partner, you meet each other's wives. If you don't do it real quick, wives get pissed. Rookie mistake number one."

"Tell her thanks, and I'll think about it."

Schilling grunted and disappeared down the hall.

James scanned his desk for anything else to keep him busy and away from home.

Mel. His eyes settled on her image, and he carefully lifted the frame. *Christmas 2013* was delicately etched in the plain silver border. His throat clenched as he rubbed his thumb over her smiling face. Their matching flannel pajamas and her shimmering Santa hat almost mocked the despair burrowed in his chest. *We were so happy. God, I wish you were still here.*

FIVE

"Bridget? Bridge? *BRIDGET?*" Frustrated, Eva ended the call and tossed the phone into her sparkly clutch. The music was too loud in the hotel bar for Eva to hear the directions her best friend tried to give. "I'll just wander about until I find her. The place isn't *that* big."

She started the trek from her car to the Ambassador Hotel and scanned her surroundings. Tulsa was like living in a bigger version of a small town. Everywhere she went, she saw someone she knew, and they talked as if no time had passed. They seemed to still know everything about each other. Sure, a lot of that could be attributed to countless hours Instagram stalking, but it made Eva feel comfortable. Tulsa was another trusted constant in her life.

The click of her mother's stylish, but uncomfortable shoes penetrated the calm and cool August night. Eva couldn't wait for fall to sweep the golden leaves from the trees. There was no better sound than the crunch of dried leaves on the streets of the city she loved. Her phone vibrated and started to sing, snapping her back to the present. Bridget's smiling picture bounced on the screen.

"Sorry I hung up on you. The only thing I could hear was the bass in the background."

"*Oh my God*, I had to go outside. I couldn't hear you at all!" Bridget said with a slight slur. "Camden hired some new deejay, Skee or Sky or Skat or something, and he's *suuuuper* loud. Tomorrow everything's going to sound like we're hearing it through cotton balls."

"Great."

"But, you know, temporary hearing loss is a small price to pay for such an amazing event. Why aren't you here yet?"

"I'm almost there. I have less than a block to go." She spun around to look at the street sign. "I just turned down Fourteenth Street."

"But I don't see you. Did you finally get a new car and not tell me?"

"Like my mom would ever cosign for that," she joked. "No, I'm walking. I had to park forever away."

"Because you're shit at parallel parking."

"I am. I'm total shit at parallel parking."

"You are worthless at parking."

"I don't even deserve to parking live."

"Yeah, you fucking suck at parking. What a nightmare. It's an absolute must that we go over parallel parking one-o-one, because apparently you missed that day, like a decade ago in driver's ed." Bridget giggled uncontrollably.

"You're entirely too honest when you drink," Eva said.

"Wait, I see you. Turn around!"

Eva watched Bridget drop the phone from her ear and turn. "Finally!" Bridget squealed and trotted over to Eva, meeting her with outstretched arms. "You're looking hot. Now, let's get shots and find you a man."

She squeezed Eva, her blond curls muffling a response. "Thanks, but I don't need a man. I don't have time to start anything right now."

"No one is talking about starting anything. We need to get you laid so you can unclench a little. You're always so uptight and roboty at parties until you relax. But that's nothing a good old fashioned roll in the sheets, or on the floor, or in the elevator can't fix." Bridget's sharp alcohol breath made Eva's eyes burn. "Before you say no, at least check out the prospects." She opened the door to The Chalkboard, the hotel's restaurant and bar. Music electrified the hair on the back of Eva's neck, and the powerful bass made the inside of her chest tickle with the rhythm. Strangers squeezed by Eva, knocking her into barstools littering the edge of the dance floor. Bridget grabbed her hand and pulled her into the crowd. A man in a too-tight shirt rubbed his body against hers, brushing his hand against her ass. She inched back to give him room to pass, but he stayed pressed against her, nodding like they shared some kind of secret.

Bridget threw her arms up in the air, pouted her lips, and moved her hips in slow, sexy circles. "Relax," she mouthed.

Eva tried to mimic her and sway with the crowd, but felt like she was impersonating a pouting toddler. Maybe she did need a drink and a one-night stand.

"Look!" Bridget's yell was barely audible over the remix of Maroon 5's newest pop song. Eva followed her friend's outstretched finger, and her gaze landed on a gaggle of half-naked gyrating women. Her face scrunched, and she looked back at Bridget.

"No, not them. *Him!*"

Eva's eyes grew to alien size when she finally saw the person Bridget pointed to.

Spencer.

Eva couldn't even count the number of times she'd made up excuses to walk by the Kappa Alpha fraternity house on campus in hopes that Spencer would be hanging out outside (and preferably shirtless). That had been during her first sophomore year of college. Since then, and an additional attempt at making it to junior status, they'd had two classes together. One each semester. Almost 365 days of meaningless flirtation. Now that she thought about it, she sounded a tad bit obsessed. *But he was really flirty the last few times we talked. He even said that we should go out soon. I'm not obsessed, just persistent.*

"Go!" Bridget said, her mouth pressed against Eva's ear. "Look how big his feet are." She gave Eva a slight push in Spencer's direction.

Eva inhaled deeply, trying to calm herself. *You can totally do this. Just have a conversation. Smile and nod. Smile and nod. Simple. He can't even really hear you in here.*

Eva flipped her hair, rolled her shoulders back, sucked in her stomach, and walked toward her crush.

"Spencer! Hi!" she shouted, even though barely two feet separated them.

"Hey, Eva!" He bent down and hugged her tight against his chest, picking her up a couple inches off the ground. With the side of his face pressed against hers, he spoke into her ear. "Come up to the lobby. I want to talk to you."

Eva felt like her stomach was going to fall out of her butt. They weren't supposed to go somewhere and talk.

They were supposed to scream over the music at each other, maybe have a drink, and then Eva would spend the rest of the weekend on the phone with Bridget analyzing every syllable uttered and deciding whether or not to text him first.

Spencer took her hand and led her up the narrow staircase to the hotel lobby, and Eva couldn't help but feel a little warmer than she had when she first arrived. She glanced over her shoulder before disappearing from the room. Bridget sat giggling at the cute bartender and hadn't noticed Eva's success.

"God, it's loud in there." Spencer's voice interrupted the photomontage of their soon-to-be romance Eva had busily created in her head. He closed the door separating the hotel from the restaurant. The sudden silence made Eva fidget with a stray thread dangling from her clutch.

"You know, I hate that we don't have any classes together anymore." Spencer reached over and brushed her hair back and off of her shoulder. He let his hand linger and slowly slide down her arm.

Goose bumps dotted Eva's skin, and her heart fluttered in her chest. "Really?" She bit her bottom lip, hoping she'd hid the shock from her voice.

"Definitely. You were the only girl who wasn't glued to her phone, and whenever I walked in, I got to see that amazing smile."

Happiness warmed her and she let her amazing smile beam.

"Actually, speaking of phones, I need to get your number." He reached for his back pocket, and his forehead wrinkled with confusion. "Damn, I must have left it in the room," he said, patting the remaining pockets of his jeans.

"A few of us got rooms on the same floor so we won't have to worry about driving or anything."

"That totally makes sense." She tried not to sound too impressed by his small act of responsibility.

"Are you staying with Bridget?"

"I hadn't planned on it," Eva said, waiting anxiously for his next question. *Is he going to ask me to stay with him?*

Instead, Spencer looked around the lobby, as if sizing it up. "Yeah, I think your friend Bridget has one too. She was talking to the check-in lady when I was getting my key."

"She didn't say anything about it, but we didn't really get a chance to talk before—"

"Before I stole you away." Spencer flashed a perfect grin. "I meant it when I said that we should go out sometime. But I have to go up to the room first to grab my phone. Want to come up with me? It'll just take a second." He walked to the elevator and Eva followed, hesitantly.

She twirled the loose thread and weighed her options. *Either go back downstairs and get groped by guys I don't even know, or go upstairs and possibly get groped by Spencer.* A smile crept across her face. "Yeah, I'll go up with you."

"I won't keep you away from the party for too long." He leaned over and pushed the up arrow.

"That's okay. I'd rather be with you."

He slid his well-toned arm behind her and pulled her close. "I feel the same way."

She held her breath and waited for his lips to press against hers.

Ding! The elevator blared, interrupting the moment.

Spencer stepped back and gestured toward the open doors. "After you."

Eva leaned into him and tried not to stare at his sizeable shoes during the short ride up to the fourth floor. As they approached the door to his hotel room, Spencer pulled the key card from his back pocket. Lint speckled the shiny cream card, and he wiped in on his shirt before sliding it into the lock.

"We should have done this sooner." The door clicked open and he motioned for her to follow him inside. "You and me together just makes sense."

"You're right." Eva laughed softly. "This is totally embarrassing, but I've wanted to talk to you, like *really* talk to you, for over a year."

"Well, we're here now." He gently took her hand and spun her around like a ballerina before pulling her closer. "What do you want to talk about?"

A girlish smile covered her lips and butterflies sprang to life in her stomach.

Spencer gripped her arms in his strong hands. "I can think of a few things. Like how beautiful you looked every day in class." He lifted her chin and brought their lips together. The rich, pine scent of his body filled the air, and she inhaled deeply. "Or how sexy you look in that dress."

She relaxed into his kiss, allowing his tongue to explore hers.

"You look so perfect every time I see you." He pressed his open palm against her back and lifted her off the ground. She wrapped her legs around his thick torso, and felt him step forward until the door was firmly behind her. Body heat radiated through her hands as her fingers outlined the taut muscles of his back. The weight of his body pinned her to the door, and she struggled against him to catch her breath.

"Spencer, I—"

"Shhh. You don't have to talk. I know what you want." His hand slithered up her thigh, forcing her dress up over her hips.

She pushed against his chest. "It's not that."

He pulled back and shot her a confused look that quickly turned irritated. "What's the problem?"

"Just slow down. Okay?"

He nodded his head. "Yeah, we have all night." He pressed his mouth against hers, and Eva once again relaxed. His hands moved around her breasts, then lowered and lifted her dress again. Eva broke the kiss and pushed him away.

"I want to go back to the party."

"It's a little too late for that." His fingers dug deeper into her as he groped around for her panties.

Fear fluttered in her chest. "Stop! You're hurting me!"

She kicked at the empty air behind him and pushed against his chest with all of her strength.

"Quit being such a fucking tease," he grunted.

She slid her hands to his face and clawed at the stubble on his cheeks. Skin bunched under her fingernails and he shoved her arms away.

"Ouch! Goddammit! You bitch!" He stepped back, covering his face with his hands. "What the fuck is wrong with you?"

Eva grabbed her clutch from where it rested on the floor and burst from the room out into the carpeted hallway.

Before she got any farther, Spencer grabbed her arm and tugged her backward. "Babe, really? C'mon. I didn't mean to call you a bitch."

"Let go of me!" She flicked his hand from her wrist and

hurried to the elevators.

"Eva, you're embarrassing yourself. What's your deal?" Spencer followed her, his tone growing more hostile.

"I don't have a *deal*. I just said no. Repeatedly." She smashed the down arrow and waited impatiently for the elevator to rescue her.

"Whatever. You came up to my room with me, and you definitely knew what was going to happen, but..."

Eva puffed as a rush of anger distracted her panic, and she wished she had the power to knock him on his ass. "You're right. It's my fault for thinking you weren't going to attack me. So sorry. Won't happen again."

She stepped into the open elevator and held her breath until the doors closed on her crush-turned-douchebag's astonished face.

"Just breathe. Everything is fine now." She straightened the skirt of her wrinkled dress and wiped away the tears flooding her eyes. "That was way close."

She took one more deep breath before the elevator door dinged. Eva tiptoed into the lobby, hoping she wouldn't run into Bridget making a last call dash to the hotel bar. She didn't have the strength to fake happiness, and she also didn't want to ruin her best friend's night. With no squealing friend in sight, she relaxed, pulled her car key from her clutch, and made her way into the quiet Tulsa night.

Eva began to regret "borrowing" her mom's designer shoes as she walked, with her toes pinched and heels blistered, down Main Street to her car.

"Couldn't parallel park *under* a street light. Had to park in a pull-through space off in the dark. But at least I'm out of there and away from Spencer." She sniffled back the last of her tears and dug for her phone to text Bridget.

Omw home. Call me later. Lots of Spencer stuff to talk about. He's such an ass! Be safe. Love you!

Distracted by her phone, she felt less uneasy about the dark trek to her car. "Let's see who's posted pictures from the party." Before she clicked the app's box, she stopped. A shape teetered on the brink of her peripheral vision. She stood on the sidewalk, frozen by panic.

Clunk, clunk. Clunk, clunk. Then a pause. They had to be footsteps. Maybe it was Spencer, pissed off and coming to get what he thought he was owed.

All the ways she could have avoided the terror building inside of her pummeled her thoughts. *I should have just crashed in Bridget's room. Or never have gone up with him in the first place.*

Without looking back, Eva wrangled her fear and sprinted toward the safety of her car. She had only gone a few steps when her pace slowed because of the pain of her shoes. Their rough straps rubbed raw on her toes and heels, and she hopped awkwardly down the street. Luckily, her silver Chevy Spark was only feet in front of her. She threw open the door and yanked it closed. Eva held her breath and looked in the driver's side mirror.

"You've got to be kidding me." An empty water bottle lazily tripped down the street and passed her car, creating the *clunk, clunk* she escaped. Dread released her stomach and she laughed with relief. "Wow. Now *that* was totally embarrassing. I'm so glad no one was out here to see me."

Her hands still shook from the encounter with the killer bottle, and she wrung them out, trying to take in deep mouthfuls of air to calm herself.

"And you didn't even lock the car doors. *So stupid.* What

if someone was really chasing you? He could've just hopped in the passenger seat. And then I'd be trapped in this little box with some lunatic. I can't believe I'm going to say this, but I really need to start listening to my mother." She tossed her clutch on to the passenger seat and began quoting her mother aloud. "Eva, park under streetlamps. It's safer. Always lock your car doors. It's safer."

A slick voice laughed softly from behind her. "Always check the backseat. It's safer."

Eva began to scream.

SIX

"How do we wake him? Oh, it must have been too much. We should have warned him. Allowed him time to prepare." Worry fueled Maiden's tone, and she manically twirled the ends of her long hair.

Mother knelt next to her sisters in a huddle above Alek. "Give him a quick slap. Something real his mind can follow."

"No! Do not hurt him!" Maiden shouted.

"Do not hurt him?" Crone puffed out a short burst of air in Maiden's direction. "He is a powerful immortal. He will hardly notice a swift slap from my withered hand." She coiled back her hand in preparation for a speedy strike.

"I'm fine, Mothers," Alek grumbled, blinking the blur from his eyes. "There's no need for concern. Or a smack."

"As I said, a powerful immortal." Crone slowly came to her feet. "Now, to more important matters. We must check on the future Oracle."

Maiden gave Alek her hand, and he pulled himself to his feet. His chest felt tight and tired, but he also sensed a new energy surging through him. "What is this?" He placed a calloused hand over his heart. "I feel, *different*."

"Come, my son. You will understand soon enough." Mother gestured for him to follow.

They disappeared into one of Tartarus's many caves. The empty black hole had once been a bright and vibrant hall. During childhood, the Furies told him many stories of the Hall of Echoes. The magnificent tales formed vivid images within his mind, and as he walked into the black, his imagination took hold.

A path of worn salt crystals, colored in a rosy pink of human flesh, dissected the hall and sapphire pools lined the cave walls, reflecting massive candlelit chandeliers. Their flickering light illuminated the beige rocks, making them glow a soft gold. Looking in each pool was looking into a moment in time. They acted as the Furies' direct link to the Mortal Realm, levels of the Underworld, and how they checked on him during his training. Soft popping under his feet jarred him from his daydream.

He shook his head, releasing made-up images of the past. Bioluminescent insects twitched on the ground beneath his shoes. He followed their greenish orbs of light as they led him down the once beautiful path and to the only remaining pure waters of Tartarus.

In the vast black, the Galazoneri stood as a beacon of hope for their dying home. The turquoise pool appeared alive and sentient as it rippled and shone bright in the windless dark. Mother, Maiden, and Crone circled the timeless waters and placed their fingertips in its beauty.

Alek stood still and silent behind his mothers. He tensed his broad back against the uncertainty writhing within him.

I am the Immortal Warrior of Tartarus. He reminded himself. *There is no task at which I will not succeed.*

Water spun around the women's fingers. The mini whirlpools grew wider and wider with every breath they took. Each underwater tornado swallowed its neighbor until only one enormous spinning pool remained. The Furies removed their fingers from the well and waited. Beads of water detached from the spinning pool and floated up. They moved slowly at first, as every drop waited for the previous to reach its destination. Then, more quickly, as hundreds of droplets wiggled up, binding together to form inchoate shapes. The spin of the pool slowed as the shape took form. Arms sprouted from the large ball of pulsing water, then legs, and a head. The water in the basin stilled, but remained bright and illuminated the liquid figure floating above. Details rippled to the surface, and Alek recognized it as Atropos, one of the three Fates, and sister to the Furies.

"Ah, sisters, it has been long since we have spoken." Atropos's creaky voice exited her watery silhouette.

Crone spoke first. "You are well, my sister?"

"Always." A smirk lifted the corners of her mouth. "My work keeps me young."

"Indeed, it has been too long. I had almost forgotten how you enjoy the task you perform."

"Yes. Still the only being with the power to cut the thread of life." Her smiled widened. "A task of which I shall never grow weary."

"And for that, you will always be my favorite of the Fates," Alek chuckled.

"Alek? You cannot possibly be the grown man I see. Come closer."

He moved forward and stood in between Crone and Maiden. "I assure you, I am the same Alek."

"The same?" she scoffed.

"I have not called on you since I was a boy and many changes have taken hold since then. But my purpose will stay true. In this task, and all others, I will forever protect the Underworld." Speaking his purpose aloud eliminated all doubt, and he relaxed into his place beside his mothers.

"It is remarkable how far you have come. I have great faith in you, Warrior."

He nodded respectfully. "Your words are much appreciated, Atropos."

"You spoke of a task. I assume this call is for more than just reminiscing."

"You are correct, sister," Mother said. "We have called upon you for a pressing matter."

"We must know more about the descendant of Pythia," Crone added.

"If you wish to dive straight into the muck, I suppose we will do so. I shall return in a moment." Alek stared into Atropos's eyes, not wanting to miss what he knew was coming. Her eyelids fluttered rapidly and each iris disappeared as they rolled backward and into her head. Her nostrils flared, and the tendons in her neck flexed tight. Her chest expanded, and when her lungs were full, the watery body relaxed and her eyes continued their circle, rolling back into place.

"It is fortunate you called upon me so soon. The timeline of the Mortal Realm's new Oracle has skipped ahead."

Maiden spoke for the first time during the call, "Skipped ahead? What is meant by this?"

"Time is a shifty beast. It does not have a set beginning or end, nor does it travel in one simple line as mortals have convinced themselves. Instead, it curves and splits, branching out below the surface like tree roots. A simple glance in the wrong direction, a misstep on the path, an ill choice of companion, and the future is new. *Eva's* future is new. Death will reach her soon. I will be left with no choice but to cut her cord and end her life," Atropos explained.

"Oh, Alek." Tears flooded Maiden's eyes. "You must leave now and find her. The Oracle and warrior together is the only hope our home and the Mortal Realm have. You must get to her in time to save her life. Without the two of you united, Tartarus will be lost and all human innocence will be wiped from their realm."

He wrapped a comforting arm around Maiden. "Atropos, can you lengthen her life? Allow me more time to search for this, Eva."

Water sloshed back and forth with the shake of her head. "I haven't the power to influence time. I only react to its commands."

"How am I to find one person in the billions that reside in the Mortal Realm?"

Mother approached him and placed her palm on the middle of his chest. "Let the new power inside you be your guide. It knows its true place and will search for the new Oracle. You must only trust yourself. You *will* find her."

He put his hand over hers and squeezed it gently. "Thank you."

Mother stepped back to rejoin her sisters. "It is all in you, my son."

"Now go, Warrior. And remember, I will be looking

after you." Atropos's smile reappeared before her watery body collapsed into the basin with a splash.

"Gather 'round," Crone urged the two women. "Alek, where is your talisman? We must recharge it with enough power so you are able to make it to the Mortal Realm and back home."

He felt around the collar of his shirt before pulling on the thin leather cord around his neck. "Here." He let go of the leather. The crystal talisman bounced against his chest and glistened in the light from the Galazoneri.

"You must be gentle with this, my son. It is dear to me. It is the only one of Tartarus's crystals that has not been tainted by the curse." Maiden's face remained wet with tears. "We have imbued it with the last of our realm's magic, beauty, power, and light."

Alek looked down at the talisman. The soft pink crystal looked like an icicle wrapped in delicate silver thread. "I will keep it close."

"Remember, the power to find the Oracle and end this curse is within you," Mother said. "But you must do it before the final pool in the Hall of Echoes drains completely. With so much evil freed, we must not be left blind to the happenings in the Mortal Realm."

"I am ready," he assured her. "I will find her and put an end to this."

Crone covered the talisman with her hand, followed by Mother's, then Maiden's. Together, Mother, Maiden, and Crone spoke. "We shall see you soon, my son."

SEVEN

Eva's screams were outmatched by the beating of her heart. It ferociously pounded against her ribcage and filled her ears with rhythmic pulsing.

"What do you want? You can have my keys, my wallet." She tossed her keys, and they landed next to her clutch in the passenger seat. "I don't have much money. Take it. I won't tell anyone." Her voice shook and cracked as she choked back tears.

"I don't want your money or your car." He surprised her with his calm and friendly tone. "I just want to spend some time with you, Eva. You know, talk. Get to know you a little bit better." He slid his hand along the driver's side door until his fingers found the lock. It clicked into place, and Eva flinched with the sound. "I hear there might be a boy or two at this party that you're interested in. But I can see why you don't want to invest too much time in any of them. It's just like the men of your generation to let you walk to your car alone at night."

Her breathing became more erratic as she spoke. "H...
How do you know my name?"

His pants scraped against the backseat as he brought
himself closer to her. "I know your family very well.
Intimately, actually." The interior of her car shrunk with
every word he uttered. "You know, a relationship doesn't
need to lead to marriage for it to be successful. I've had a
lot of very successful relationships. I could give you some
advice if you're interested."

His voice sounded familiar, but her thoughts raced and
she couldn't place it. Instead, she focused on the image in
the rearview mirror. He lunged forward. Eva's entire body
clenched, and she squeezed her eyes shut. "No, then, on
the advice? Well, maybe later, after you've gotten a bit more
comfortable." His fingers gently combed the ends of her
tangled hair. "This a new color?"

Eva sobbed and shook her head side to side. "Please,
don't. I'll do whatever you want."

"It's okay." His rough finger wiped at the tears streaming
down her cheek. "I like it, don't worry. It looks very natural."

"Please don't hurt me. Please don't hurt me."

"Eva, what have I done to make you think I want to
harm you right now? I've been nice. Asked questions about
your night and given you compliments. I even offered you
advice. That's a lot more than most fathers do these days.
I know your father is out of the picture. I thought you'd
appreciate this."

Thoughts flew erratically through her mind. She knew
she only had a limited amount of time to free herself. Slowly
and without moving the rest of her body, she walked her
fingers to the window control levers on the door. She felt

around for the raised edge of the door lock control pad. Without hesitation, she pushed the unlock button. With the command, all of the locks popped up as they released. Eva pulled away from her assailant and, leaning all of her weight on her car door, she tore at the handle and pushed it open. Her knee smacked the pavement as she fell sideways out of the car and onto the street. She scrambled to her feet and hobbled away from her car.

Poorly lit office buildings lined the street, all closed for the long weekend. The road was empty of cars and foot traffic, and it seemed like miles to the lively party she'd just left. Streetlamps sparsely dotted the sidewalk, each only casting a small circular patch of light on the ground below. Downtown Tulsa had never looked so dark and dead.

"Help!" Eva sobbed as the city she loved turned its back on her.

The car door creaked open behind her, and his shoes hit the pavement with a soft thud. "Eva, what are you doing? Weren't we close to reaching some kind of common ground? I may not be as hip and young as you, but I think I'm okay. Nothing to run away from, that's for sure," he called.

The stiff shoes she'd taken from her mom made it impossible for her to gain any ground, and she tripped and fell to the concrete before reaching the curb. Two sets of straps came up from the sole of the shoe and wrapped around each ankle, secured in place by a small buckle. Her hands shook wildly as she dug at her feet to unclasp them, but the rigid straps only squeezed her feet tighter. "Please, please, please," she begged before abandoning the effort to free herself from the bulky shoes.

Gravel dug under her fingernails as she clawed the street

with her hands. Fighting the stiffness and pain in her knee, she crawled forward. Small rocks bore through the thin skin of her knees, leaving behind bloody craters.

His shoes grazed the ground with each step. The scratching sound of his soles on the street got louder as he marched closer. Her limbs shook as hope drained from her body.

Tears dripped into her open mouth. "Somebody help me!" Her raw throat felt like it would bleed from her screams. "Please!"

No one came to her defense. Tulsa's vacant night remained black and still.

"Shhh, it's entirely too late for you to be so loud." His thick shadow crept over her body. "Settle down. Eva, this is happening and it's not a bad thing."

Her teeth chattered uncontrollably, and she clamped her mouth shut to keep from biting her tongue.

His shoes stopped next to her, and his shadow felt heavy across her back. "Will you roll over for me? Please? It's hard to have a conversation with the back of your head."

She complied and rolled to her back. His image blurred through her tears, and she blinked rapidly to clear her eyes.

"There. That's better, isn't it?" He crouched down next to her and examined her knees. "They look pretty bad. We'll have to clean them up so they don't get infected. Don't want you all scraped and dirty before we even get home." He gently brushed away the gravel embedded in her knees.

Eva kicked and felt the power of another burst of adrenaline surge through her body. "Don't touch me!" she shrieked and flailed her arms toward the face of her hooded attacker. Desperately, she scratched and dug at whatever her fingers touched. She pulled at the fabric of his sweatshirt before he turned his face away.

"I'm trying to help you," he said, wrapping his hand around her swollen knee. He gripped her joint and pushed it toward the concrete. Eva let out a sharp squeal and recoiled.

"This played out so much differently in my head," he said with a sigh. "Can I share something with you?" His grasp tightened around her knee. "I thought we would share some kind of connection, you know? Now I feel a little foolish. But I guess that's why you shouldn't make up what first meetings are going to be like. They never quite live up to your expectations."

The muscles in the back of Eva's knee stretched under his weight. She tightened her jaw and readied herself for the excruciating pain.

"That's kind of how I felt the first time I met Lori."

The mention of her mother flooded Eva with fear, and she forced her body to still.

"My mom?" The words came out as tiny squeaks.

"That's right. I know so much about you." He cleared his throat. "Now, what do you want to do about this little situation we're in?"

"I'll stop."

He released his grip on her leg. "Thank you. You *are* everything Lori said you'd be." The dark hid his face, but she heard a smile in his voice. "Now, we need to get you off of this dark, dirty street and someplace safe. How does that sound?"

Okay. She mouthed the word, but couldn't get her voice to leave her body.

"Excellent." He rose to his feet and offered her his

hand. "Take it. It's not going to bite."

Eva pressed her back into the pavement and prayed for it to open up and swallow her whole.

"Didn't we sort this out? You do what I say, and I won't make veiled threats against your mom. I think I'm being reasonable." His shoes creaked as he crouched back down to her side.

She nodded and gave him a shaking arm. He grabbed it around the wrist and yanked her to her feet.

"Ahh!" She howled as pain cut through her body. "My knee." She stood on one leg, bending the other knee to keep her weight off of it.

"I know. Just try to fight through it. Pain builds character."

"I can't," she whispered, tears streaking her face.

"That's okay. It's something that builds over time." He crouched down, threading his arm under hers. He pulled her against his chest before bending down to scoop up her legs into his free arm. Her stomach churned, and the contents threatened to fly out of her mouth as his musky scent wafted up her nose.

He carried her over to the passenger side of the car and grunted as he balanced her weight to unlatch the car door. The car's dome light flashed on, and he slowly lowered her onto the passenger seat. "There's always so much crap in girls' cars," he said collecting the items she'd thrown on the seat.

With his body stretched across hers, he fastened her seatbelt. "Safety first, as they say."

Eva's eyes met his. The light illuminated his face as he removed himself from the car.

"Bill?" she croaked. Fresh tears filled her eyes with

prickly heat.

"Eh, more or less." He brushed off the question and made sure her appendages were securely in the car before shutting the door.

Bill climbed into the driver's seat, fastened his seatbelt, and turned the key in the ignition.

"Bill, why are you doing this?" Eva's voice came out so hushed she didn't know if he heard her.

He adjusted the rearview mirror before he spoke. "I really didn't think you'd be that surprised to see me. You had to know everything your ancestors did would eventually catch up with you."

Eva thought back to what she knew about her family. "I…I don't understand."

"Eva, you can trust me. You may think you can't, but you can. I realize how absurd it sounds, but I'm actually the good guy here." He laughed loudly. Eva tried joining him, but it came out hollow and hoarse. "You don't have to play the whole Midwest girl act. Better yet." He lifted his hips and fished something out of the front pocket of his pants. "These are for you. They'll help with any pain and make it easier for you to sleep. It is important that you remain alert tomorrow, not nodding off." He held his hand out in front of her face. Two small blue oval pills rested in his palm.

Eva shook her head and pushed her body into the corner between her seat and the door. "I don't want those. I'll be good. I promise."

"It's not about you being good. It's about you being comfortable." He pinched the pills between the index finger and thumb of his other hand and pressed them to her tightly pursed lips. Eva grunted against the pressure of his fingers, determined to not let the pills into her mouth. Bill let out an annoyed sigh and grabbed under her cheekbones with his free thumb on one side and remaining four fingers on the other. He squeezed and pulled her face closer to the center of the car. Her body followed unwillingly. He again forced the pills against her mouth. Eva couldn't fight his strength and her lips parted. His salty fingers pushed between her teeth and dropped the pills on her tongue. Their bitterness made her gag. He pinched closed her nose and the flesh around her lips. "Chew before you swallow, Eva. They'll work faster that way."

She chewed until the pills disintegrated into a foul tasting paste. He let go of her face and Eva gasped. Bill reached into the backseat and brought back a bottle of water. One of many that Eva had left there.

"Those probably don't taste very good. Here, wash them down. You should start to feel better very soon." A smile sliced his face. Eva averted her eyes and leaned her head on the passenger window.

The car pulled onto the street as she watched her reflection in the side mirror. The pills took hold, and her body felt like heavy mush. She pictured herself giving up, dissolving into a puddle of despair, and splashing onto the floorboard. She tried to combat the cloudiness cloaking her thoughts.

What has my family done? What have I done to deserve this? No answers appeared, and Eva let the passing white street lines lull her to sleep.

EIGHT

Alek's heart fluttered with excitement as his mothers filled the talisman with enough energy for a round trip journey to the Mortal Realm and, hopefully, enough time while there to fulfill his mission. He took a deep, calming inhale and readied himself for transportation. If only landing his body was as simple as locating the nearest runway. During his training, he hadn't quite figured out how to make any of his arrivals exact, something his pride wouldn't allow him to reveal to his mothers. They repeatedly told him the key was concentration, and that he must allow his entire being to fill with thoughts of his destination. Unfortunately, fantasies of battle and locking up the evil he had trained to destroy always seeped through, clouding his focus at the last moment.

"I cannot allow anything to shift my focus." His jaw clenched with determination. "Eva, Eva. My thoughts are with Eva." He let his voice fade to a whisper, repeating his mantra on an internal loop. The air crackled around him as the heaviness of his mothers' hands and the firmness of the ground below his feet began to fade.

His extremities tingled with anticipation. *This is where your true journey begins. You will succeed, and your home will be restored.*

His heartbeat quickened as warm air encircled his body and pinpricks of electricity popped off his skin. *All of Tartarus's escaped evil will learn to fear you as one by one they are destroyed and sent back to their cells to rot.* He clenched and unclenched his fists.

The force of him tearing through to the Mortal Realm electrified the air of his new surroundings. Like a comet, he burned through the cushion protecting one realm from the next. The space around him illuminated and forced its way through his closed eyelids.

His hand flew to his talisman. "Eva!" he shouted, trying to force his destination back on track.

Metal slammed into his back. The impact forced the air out of his lungs and made his vision spin.

"Fuck me," he croaked. Chunks of glass snuck into his pants as he hefted his butt out of a destroyed sunroof. He rolled out of the large crater and over the mangled metal. "I fucking hate cars," he mumbled, flopping to the pavement. Glass and pieces of plastic dug into his back.

He caught his breath and hefted himself off of the ground. He brushed beads of glass from his hair and studied the perimeter for bystanders. The night remained still, and he walked briskly away from the totaled sedan.

"David L. Moss Criminal Justice Center?" The white stone sign loomed at the edge of the parking lot. "Criminal Justice Center? Why would Eva be here?" He wrinkled his brow and brushed more debris from his shoulders. "I did this. Thinking of my coming victory instead of focusing on the task at hand." Anger swelled in his chest. "Think, Alek. You have been given the tools to find her, now do it."

He clasped the talisman and mindlessly rubbed his thumb over its smooth silver thread. "Tartarus and the Mortal Realm are depending on you."

Trust yourself. Mother's words snaked into his thoughts. *Let the new power inside you be your guide. It will search for the new Oracle.* He calmed and relaxed into her guidance. *You must only trust yourself.*

"Thank you, Mother," he whispered before tucking the amulet into his shirt.

He focused on the new power tickling his lungs. "Eva, find Eva. Find the Oracle. She is your true master." Pain bit at his chest as the magic swirling in his body roared to life. "Lead me to her."

The power surged with an aching ferocity, pulling him down empty streets until he reached a set of large glass doors. An awning stretched overhead with the words Ambassador Hotel written in thin swooping letters.

"This looks more promising than David L. Moss," Alek muttered to himself. He stepped through the open doors and followed signs pointing him to the guest services desk. His time in the Mortal Realm thus far had taught him that people who stood behind desks usually had some answers, and ideally were the ones he sought.

"Hi, welcome to the Ambassador Hotel. Are you checking in?" The petite woman standing behind the counter asked with a pleasant smile.

"No, I am here to find a woman."

The attendant's smile faded. "Sir, I don't think I can

help you. We're not that kind of establishment."

"Oh. Wait, no. That's not what I meant." Alek blushed. "I know the woman I'm looking for. Her name is Eva. I am almost certain she is here."

The clerk put up her pale hand, signaling for him to stop. "I'm sorry, but I still can't help you. I'm not allowed to give out guests' room numbers. If you know the full name her reservation is under, I can call the room for you. But it is after two thirty in the morning. Unless she's with the party that moved up to the fourth floor, I don't think she'll be awake to answer."

"The party?" Alek swallowed against the heat in his chest.

"Yes. A few students from the university bought out the restaurant. There was a new deejay. And lots of drinking." She frowned and scrunched her tiny nose like she smelled something unpleasant. "It was all very loud."

"I'll go to the fourth floor and make sure she's not there. How do I...?" He pointed to the ceiling.

"Get to the fourth floor?" she asked, her smile reappearing. "Just walk down the hall behind you, and you'll see the elevators on your right."

"Elevators?" Alek asked.

"Yes, they'll be on your right. Have a wonderful morning." She turned from him to assist another guest.

Alek followed her directions and weaved between groups of beer-soaked partygoers taking pictures of themselves. He reached the end of the hall and stared blankly at the two banks of elevators. "Up," he said. After a minute he tried again. "Up, please?" The left bank of elevator doors immediately opened.

"For shit's sake, Jill. Did you not push the goddamn button? No wonder we've been standing here for so fucking long."

Alek peered into the open box, and the two young women inside eyeballed him. "Will this take me to the fourth floor?"

"Totes!" the girl closest to him chimed.

"Totes, Jill? Seriously? What are you, like, sixteen?" The snippy blond cleared her throat before continuing. "Yes, this will take you to the fourth floor. It's such a coincidence, that's actually where we're going." Her voice lightened as she spoke to Alek. "Get in!"

Alek stepped in between the doors and awkwardly waited for whatever happened next.

"No, come closer, silly." She waved him to her. "The doors won't close if you stand right in their way."

Alek walked to her; the thick steel doors came together behind him.

"Thank you for saving ussss?" She stretched out the last word and emphasized her question by raising an eyebrow.

"My name is Alek."

She pulled a bottle from behind her back and took a swig. Clear liquid dribbled down her chin and onto her strapless top. Her pastel pink sequin skirt started above her bellybutton and hugged her thin frame. Alek couldn't tell if her skirt was supposed to be that high, or if it had ridden up without her noticing.

"It's a pleasure to meet you, Alek." She offered him her best smile. "I'm Bridget. You want?" She held out the bottle. Absolut Raspberry was written in big pink letters across the frosted glass.

"No, I'm okay." He leaned away from the bottle. "I don't like alcohol."

"Had a bad experience?"

Alek nodded. "A woman I met in Segovia bought me a drink. The bartender lit it on fire, and my next memory is waking up hours later with singed eyebrows."

"Oh, yeah I've done that before. You have to blow those out first." She paused to take another gulp. "But that's okay. I'm not really much of a drinker either." Using the elevator to brace herself, she slid across the mirror-lined wall until she was close enough for him to smell the liquor clinging to her breath and clothes. "Thank you for saving us, Alek." Her tongue grazed her top teeth as she enunciated each syllable of his name.

His stomach lurched, and he tilted his head up to breathe in the clean air above her.

"Yeah, thanks for rescuing us, Alek," Jill chimed in.

"Jill, shut your mouth and push the fucking button so we can get out of this box!" Bridget snapped. She flipped her hair, took another drink, and turned back to Alek. She leaned closer, pressing her chest into his arm as she spoke. "And into someplace a little more comfortable. I'm all alone in room 419. If you're not busy, you could be." She stepped back and sloppily traced the outline of her body with her free hand.

"Perhaps on a different day."

The elevator doors opened with a ding, and Bridget hooked Alek's arm with hers, dragging him past Jill and into the hallway.

"Don't be silly. You can come in for just one drink." She raised the bottle and shook it in the air. "I'm sure the girl who's waiting on you won't care."

"No one is waiting on me. I—"

"Perfect!" she interrupted. "And looky! My room. Excellent timing." She released his arm and propped herself up against the wall while she pushed her room key in and out of the door slot.

"Bridget, there is something much more important I must to do. I can't—"

"Shhhhhhhh." She shoved a sticky finger over his mouth. "Fine. Whatever. But can you make this card thingy open the door?" She slipped the key into his hand. "Whenever I do it, it gets all red and flashy at me."

She unscrewed the bottle cap to take another sip before shuffling over to make room for him at the door. Alek copied off her and carefully slid the key into the opening. The lock made a whirring sound and a green button illuminated.

"Have a good night." He propped the door open with his foot and turned to give the key back. Bridget wrapped her arms around his neck and pressed her lips to his. The sudden movement tangled their feet, and she fell backward into the hotel room. Alek landed on top of her, and the opened bottle sloshed its contents onto his neck before clattering to the floor. The door slammed shut behind them. Bridget rolled over on top of Alek and held the bottle over his face. "Have one drink," she whined. "I don't want to be the only fun one here." Alek opened his mouth to protest, and she tilted the bottle into his mouth. He coughed and sputtered. It tasted dry and sweet and burned as it washed down his throat.

"I could tell you wanted to come with me but needed a good excuse." She released her grip around his neck and stuck out her bottom lip in a flirtatious pout. "So I gave you one."

Alek's legs wobbled as he stumbled to his feet. He brushed the back of his neck with his hand and moisture dripped from his fingers.

"Oh no, you're all wet." She held her arms out for balance as she stood. "Come rinse off with me."

Unable to trust his legs, Alek staggered over to the bed.

"Whoopsie." Bridget tripped over her shoes as she kicked them off. "I may have had a teensy bit too much to drink." She giggled and swept her blond curls up into her hands. "Help me with my zipper?" She backed into him. The heat from her body warmed his tingling thighs.

"I, uh." Alek's cheeks turned red and his eyes felt like they were swimming in his head. He pawed at one of the zippers spinning in his vision.

"What is taking you so long?" Bridget dropped her hair and looked back at him. "Wait. Are you...drunk? Seriously? You're swaying around like a toddler and you barely even had one drink."

Alek shrugged his shoulders and opened his mouth to respond, but all that came out was a burp.

"Oh my God. Epic fail. And you're so cute. Shame." She stepped away from him and began the process of turning her strapless top around her body so the zipper faced front.

Alek crashed backward onto the mound of decorative pillows and watched. His thoughts spiraled and his vision blurred. "H...How are—" Hiccups interrupted his question. "How are you doing that with your body? It's all twisted all around." Hiccups intermittently halted his laugh.

"Someone must have pregamed. Why do I always get

stuck with the losers?" she grumbled. "Okay, look there's water next to the bed. Drink it and sober up a little bit. I'm going to hop in the shower. When I come back, you better be ready. You don't want to let this go to waste." She unzipped her top and it fell to the floor.

Those are nice, Alek thought before closing his eyes.

NINE

"Hey! Hey! Jesus Christ. Alek, or whatever your name is, get up!"

Alek rolled to his side and away from the person poking him. "Be gone," he grumbled. "I will wake later."

"Fine. Then you're going to have to pay for another night in this room. Check out is in like five minutes, and I'm not getting stuck paying for your lazy ass."

"Check out?" Alek opened his eyes and squinted against the sunlight pouring in from the room's picture window.

"Yeah. You passed out for like six hours off of that baby shot of Absolut. Totally ruined an otherwise fantastic night. I even had to sleep on the couch because you were all sprawled out like an enormous dead ogre. Now get up! Ándale!"

Alek sat up, panicked. "What have I done?" A dull ache pulsed behind his eyes.

"Well, let's see." Bridget took a break from packing her heels into her neon green overnight bag to tick off the list. "You embarrassed yourself by proving what a total lightweight you are. You lost your shot at ever hooking up with me. And you ruined a perfectly good throw pillow by drooling all over it."

Alek glanced down at the mound of pillows he slept on. A slick spot saturated the ivory silk, creating a puddle of beige. He flipped it over and stood up. "I have to go and find the new, uh, my friend."

"Well, that makes two of us." She dropped her bag by the door and took her phone from the pocket of her turquoise hoodie.

The skin on the back of his neck was tight, and he rubbed his hand over it. "Disgusting," he groaned. The vodka Bridget spilled on him the night before had dried into a sticky film. The raspberry stink followed him as he rushed to the bathroom.

"Sure, take your time. Go to the bathroom. Take a shower. It's not like I have anywhere to be."

Alek watched Bridget's reflection in the bathroom's mirror. She impatiently shifted her weight side to side while repeatedly pressing the call button on her phone.

"I also have somewhere more important to be." He turned on the faucet and scraped at the back of his neck with a wet hand towel, trying to remove all traces of the pungent alcohol and his growing regret.

"Come on, Eva. Pick up. I know you're awake. You wake up at, like, the crack of dawn every day," Bridget said to her phone as she dialed again.

"Eva." Alek lowered the towel and stepped out of the bathroom. "Your friend's name is Eva?"

"Umm, yeah."

"You know Eva?"

"I know *an* Eva. Me and thousands of other people. I'm pretty sure I'm not the only person who has a friend named Eva."

"But you are the only person here who knows someone named Eva."

She dropped the phone to her side. "If by *here* you mean this room, then yes."

"I came here last night looking for someone by that name, and now you are trying to find your friend Eva. This must be more than coincidence."

"I guess." She paused, studying him. "Are you that guy from her boring English seminar?"

"What? No. I don't think I even know what an English seminar is." He wrinkled his forehead and continued rubbing the syrupy mess off of his neck.

"If you think we're talking about the same person, and you're not the English seminar guy, then you have to be the one from her anthropology class. The gum popper. She said that you're super hot, but annoying. You know, because of all of the gum popping. I told her that I knew you were just doing it to get her attention, and apparently I was right. I usually am."

"I don't know her from class." Alek went back into the bathroom to rewet the towel.

She pressed a few buttons on her phone before lifting it to her ear. "Well, I can't imagine *my* Eva not telling me about you, so we're probably talking about two different people."

He came out of the bathroom and stood next to Bridget.

"It's too bad, too. Tall, blond hair, tan, muscly, those pretty honey-colored eyes, it makes a gorgeous package."

Alek puffed his chest at the string of compliments. "You're definitely her type."

"You wouldn't happen to know where she is? *Your* Eva. So I can be sure that is not who I'm looking for."

She shook her head. "Sorry. That's who I've been trying to get ahold of while you were using the sink like a birdbath. I haven't had any luck, though. She's not even answering my texts."

"Thank you for your help. I apologize for ruining your pillow." He opened the door and waited for Bridget to walk through it.

She smiled up at him. "I think housekeeping has seen worse. Especially from last night's party. Go ahead and go. I'm going to try Eva a few more times before I head down. The elevator messes with my service."

The door closed behind him, and he could hear the beeping of Bridget's phone as she attempted to call Eva again.

Alek waited impatiently in the empty hallway for the elevator to open.

The sense of urgency returned and filled him with guilt.

"Come now, elevator," he demanded, remembering this time to push the down button. He did so repeatedly until it chimed its arrival. The elevator slowly lowered to the lobby, and for the first time, Alek was glad the Hall of Echoes was barren. He didn't want his mothers to watch as he disappointed them.

The elevator stilled and Alek walked out the lobby doors and into the sunny midmorning air. Summer still had its hold on Tulsa, and the temperature outside made Alek uncomfortable and sweaty. He stood baking in the sun and waited for the power within him to pull him toward Eva.

"Why is nothing happening?" Fiery pressure burned in his chest, but the extreme pull he'd felt the night before was clouded by new thoughts of doubt and self-pity.

He plucked the talisman from under his shirt and pressed his only connection to his home between the palms of his hands. "Pythia, I again need your aid. For the first time in my life, I have no idea what to do and know of nowhere else to turn." He strengthened his hold on the talisman and concentrated on flooding the Underworld with his plea.

A familiar, chilling laughter trickled into his thoughts. *Pythia?*

"Who else would I be, Immortal Warrior of Tartarus?"

Thank you for answering my call. How is it that I can hear you?

"Your mind is young and desolate. The tentacles of my expansive power wriggled in without problem. Did you call on me to display my abilities, or is it my aid of which you are in need?" Her voice became louder and more forceful as she spoke.

I can no longer fully connect with the power that leads me to the future Oracle. Can you grant me something new so I can continue this journey?

"Young warrior, my gifts make time itself quiver and hide. But, in this, even I am void of guidance."

If even you cannot help me, what am I to do? How will I find her?

"Stop searching in others for what only you possess." Her anger boomed. "Out of your heart spark the fires of fearless confidence, yet it is now ignored by your embryonic brain. Warrior, the belief in oneself is more powerful a tool than the broadest of prayers." She left his mind with the reverberation of laughter as the only evidence of her visit.

Alek's eyelids fluttered open. "She is right. I am the Immortal Warrior of Tartarus. I haven't time to doubt myself."

He cleared his mind and stared at the speckled gray pavement between his feet.

Eva, I know I have the power to find you. I am the protector of this realm. Now, I am your protector.

The heat within his chest flared in response.

Eva, descendant of the great Oracle Pythia, I will find you. I will save you. Together, we will restore my home and rid this realm of evil.

The fire beneath his lungs roared to life, and the feeling of urgency exploded inside him. He rubbed his open hand on his chest and smiled. "Eva."

TEN

James sat on the edge of his desk and studied crime scene files and photos while he waited for Schilling. "Where the victim was last seen and where her body was found are within blocks of each other." He studied the images again before settling on the conclusion. "How did we miss this? It's so obvious."

He fished in his pocket for his phone and dialed Schilling's number. The voicemail picked up after only a couple rings. "Hey, it's me. Found something you should see. I'm waiting for you at the precinct." He ended the call and flagged down the nearest detective. "You seen Schilling anywhere?"

"Uh, yeah. He's in with the captain."

"Thanks, man." He stuffed his phone in his pocket and headed down the hall.

Before he rounded the corner to the captain's office, his phone chimed. He cleared the text message icon, and slipped it back into his pants.

Schilling's voice grumbled into the hallway. "He tattooed

her and sliced up her body. This is the real thing."

"Shit." Captain Alvarez let out a big puff of air. "We've got to put this one down fast, Schilling. Can't have the city panicking."

"I know. We'll keep the lid on it and get a solve."

"And what do you think about your new partner? Cases like this come with a lot of attention. Think he'll be able to handle it?"

They sat in silence for a moment, and James waited for Schilling's response. "He's already working on some theories. He's got the head for it..."

"But what?"

"He's young and not too into making friends."

Captain Alvarez chuckled. "From what my predecessors told me, neither were you."

"Rookie mistake number two. I learned."

"I'm telling you, Graham is straight out of Gotham. You haven't seen his military record. We're lucky he chose to join the force."

James loudly cleared his throat before turning the corner.

"Graham, perfect timing. I was just about to tell your partner here the good news. I'm putting you both as lead investigators on this case."

"That's great." Schilling stood and shook the captain's hand.

"Yes, thank you, sir. We won't let you down." James stepped forward and gave him a firm handshake.

"That's what I like to hear. See that you don't." Captain Alvarez sat back in his cushioned chair and took a sip from his coffee mug.

"Then we'll be getting back to it." Schilling led them out

of the small office and down the hall.

"I noticed something," James said as he followed his partner to the parking lot. "Our victim was last seen around two in the morning downtown at a late night pizza joint. At some point, between her leaving her friends and getting back to her apartment on campus, our perp grabbed her."

"Right, I read the file. Her roommate said that she never made it home, but they found her car at the school. No one in the area heard anything that night, and there are no cameras in the vicinity. So we don't know if the car was dumped there or if she drove and was abducted between her parking space and her front door."

They reached the car, and James climbed into the passenger seat. "It also says that her body was found two days later barely two blocks away from where she was last seen. All three of those places are too close together not to mean anything. He may not have killed her near there, but that's where he likes to hunt."

"We need to send out a report telling everyone to call us if anyone goes missing within a five mile radius of where he dropped her body," Schilling instructed.

James pulled out his phone and typed up a precinct wide e-mail. "It's sent. I hope we don't hear anything, but I doubt he'll stay away for long." He let the rest of the ride continue in silence.

The car bounced over potholes as they drove into the parking lot of the medical examiner's office. "I'm close to mixing something up and filling those holes my damn self," Schilling grumbled and pushed himself off the seat.

"Jesus Christ." He used the back of his sleeve to wipe sweat from his face. "I'm sweating buckets out here, and I haven't even walked ten feet. Fall needs to kick it into gear."

"Yeah, it's brutal." James opened the office door. Cool air rushed out, and he eagerly followed it inside.

"Ay! Tom!" A curvaceous woman threw up her hands and came out from behind the front desk. Her tall, spikey heels clacked against the tile floor as she giddily walked to the men. Her tight blue dress hugged her body, accentuating the intoxicating sway of her hips.

She stood on her tiptoes, and Shilling gave her a bear hug. "V, I thought you were going to be out for the whole year."

"Sí, I thought so too, but my brother was arrested again. My parents finally had enough. They took Gloria from him last night. So, I come to work again," she enunciated through her thick accent.

"It's good to have you back. Veronica, meet my new partner, Detective James Graham."

"Any friend of Tom's is a friend of mine." She gave him a sultry half smile. "You have come here for seeing the bodies, no?"

"Yes. We're here to see Dr. Pierce. And the bodies," James said, concentrating on the smooth angles of her face so his eyes were too busy to drift over her spandex dress.

"I'll sign you in. You go back. Have your meeting with the crypt keeper." Veronica's smile widened, and she ushered them past the first set of doors.

Pierce stood outside the exam room tapping her foot impatiently. Her petite frame was dwarfed by the width and height of the spotless hallway. "You're late. And lucky I'm still here. I have other bodies that need attention, including my own."

"Sorry, Catherine. We got held up at the station,"

James said.

"And by Veronica," Schilling whistled. "Good to see her back."

"She does give you something nice to look at after dealing with dead bodies all day. Why do you think I hired her?" Pierce winked playfully and opened the door to the exam room. "Graham, I got your message about the UV ink. You think it could be what's causing the ridges on the tattoo?"

"Sure do, but we won't know for sure until we check."

"Which is where I come in." She walked over to the wall covered in oversized silver filing cabinets. "Schilling, there's a light wand behind you. Grab it for me, and I'll pull out your victim."

She pulled open the small square door separating the living from the dead. A thin, white sheet covered the body leaving only the crown of her head exposed. Pierce lifted one side of the sheet to reveal the victim's left arm as she explained. "Kirby already ran a UV light over the body when it first came in, but that examination was to test for signs of sexual assault, which the victim tested negative for. No blood or semen on the body or the clothes. So if this ink lights up, Kirby just missed it the first time around." The dense black tattoo looked garish against her pale flesh. Pierce rotated the girl's arm so the ridges through and around the tattoo faced up.

"I'm ready when you are," she said.

Schilling clicked on the light and held it a few inches above the skin.

The UV bulb reflected a bluish white X tattooed over one of the tree limbs. Next to it was a sequence of numbers

23.8.14, and in the middle of the hollow trunk glowed the victim's last name.

"Oh God. The twenty-third of August, 2014," Pierce said without masking the horror in her voice. "Why would he tattoo her body with the date she died?"

"And next to an X on the tree? Is he trying to mark that date on the tree? It doesn't make sense." James's flicker of hope for a possible lead grew dimmer as he became more confused.

"It's ancestry," Schilling said. "The sick bastard put the X through one of these small limbs, right?" His finger hovered over the area he spoke about and, without waiting for an answer, he continued. "It's an offshoot of the Bailey family tree. He's cut off the branch. He ended that part of their family. Wait, hold that thought. I'm buzzing." Schilling handed James the UV light and put his phone on speaker.

"What do you got for us?"

"I have a note here that says you need to be alerted if any disappearances from the downtown area are called in."

"Yeah, and?" Schilling said impatiently.

"A Lori Kostas just reported her twenty-three-year-old daughter missing. Said she was downtown last night at a party, and she hasn't come home or been heard from since."

James's heartbeat quickened. "Send us the mom's address. We're headed there now."

ELEVEN

Eva rolled to her side. Heaviness tugged at her ankle, and she thrust out her leg to shake it away. Dull pain gripped her knee, and she opened her eyes to seek out the cause. She blinked hard against the thick, dry contacts fogging her vision.

"Morning. Did you sleep well? You were out like a light."

She used her elbow to prop herself up to a seated position. Her head spun with sleepiness. "Where am I?"

"At home. Well, Bill's home."

Her breath caught in her throat as her vision cleared and settled on him. Memories bolted through her and terror gripped her stomach. She sat up, brought her knees to her chest, and pressed herself against the concrete wall behind her. A thick shackle of chain was wrapped around her ankle.

"Now Eva, there's no reason to be afraid. We're just chatting. Remember, I'm one of the good guys." She followed his eyes as they looked around the room. Each concrete wall was framed with plywood and sheets of drywall leaned up against them. "I know what you're thinking, it still needs work. I've been watching a lot of those home improvement shows for ideas." He hopped on the metal exam table cemented to the floor in the middle of the room. "You know the shows I'm talking about?"

Eva's breathing quickened, and she nodded at him weakly.

"Is this scaring you?"

Eva nodded again, holding back tears.

"Just pretend it's not here. It's a table, Eva. A table can't hurt you." He rubbed his palm over the table's smooth surface. "I got this at an estate sale. I know why I need this, but I cannot for the life of me think of why those people needed it. But we don't need to focus on this right now. Okay? Tell me okay."

"Okay," she rasped.

"You don't need to use your inside voice down here, Eva. The walls are concrete. It's a fantastic sound barrier. No one can hear a peep from down here."

Eva hung her head. An oversized man's T-shirt and sweat pants draped over her body. Her eyes widened and bile roared in her stomach as she did an internal body check.

Don't freak out. Don't freak out.

Tears dripped from her eyes and speckled her light gray sweat pants.

"Nothing happened. I just rinsed you off and put you in a clean outfit. I wouldn't do anything to you while you were unconscious. That's not going to happen," he snorted. "That's not what this is about."

Eva swallowed hard and forced her eyes to relax. Her throat was sore and her voice hoarse as she spoke. "What happens now?"

"I thought that we'd pick up where we left off last night and spend some more time together. No need to rush things. Don't you agree?"

She nodded slowly.

Bill continued, "You know, I've been following your family for a while. Well, not literally following, that'd be creepy. That only started after I got out and made my way up here, but I know a lot about you, Eva. Why do you think I chose you?"

"I...I don't know. I don't know. Why did you choose me?"

"You already know the answer."

"I don't. I swear."

"It's staring at you plain as day."

"I swear I don't know. Just tell me what you want from me."

"Admit what your ancestors did for hundreds of years and this will all be over. You want to go home, don't you?"

"But I...I don't have anything to admit. They were ranchers, I think. What did they do?" She tripped over her words as her exhausted body trembled.

"For hundreds of years your ancestors spouted prophecies that resulted in the slaying of innocent beings and you want to pretend like it never happened?" He slipped off the table, took a deep breath, and exhaled slowly. "I'm not going to lie to you; I'm getting a little irritated. This game you're playing is making me very tired. And you're never going to win. I am always the victor."

"I'm not playing a game," she said meekly.

Bill crept closer to her, right at the edge of her chain. "Then why won't you admit it?" he hissed between clenched teeth.

"I don't know what you're talking about!" she screamed, tears pouring from her eyes.

"Confess your family's crimes. Accept the blame!" He took a deep breath and smoothed out his button-down shirt. "We'll both feel so much better after you do. This will all be over."

"You're not making any sense," she sobbed. "This is crazy. *You* are crazy." She buried her head in her knees and struggled to control her shaking.

"I'm a big enough man to admit that I may be, just a little. Being trapped in a pit in the Underworld for centuries will do that to you."

Eva lifted her head and let her legs dangle over the edge of the cot. "Bill, I know that you're confused. But I want to help you," she said, using the back of her hand to dry her face. "I won't say anything about what's happened. I just want to help you get better before you do anything you might regret. Please, just let me help you."

He charged at her, stopping inches from her face. She stiffened and her chest shook as she inhaled. "You're testing my patience, Eva." His breath stunk like old bandages. "I'm willing to help you, but only if you're willing to help me. Can you do that?" She nodded stiffly. "Great. We're going to have an exchange. I'll tell you something you want to hear, and then you tell me something that I want to hear. Okay?" He stood and shuffled back a few steps. "The reason your dad left you. Do you want to know what made him run?"

His eyes scanned her face, and she uttered a weak reply, "Yes."

"I did. It was me. He left because I got free. Daddy

tucked his tail and ran because he was scared. He knew I would come looking for vengeance and my hunt would lead me straight to you. He didn't want to deal with it, with you. That's why he left you, because he's a coward. And because he understood that under my caring exterior is a creature to be feared and respected. You understand that too, don't you?"

Bill's phone rang and Eva felt a sliver of relief as he pulled it out of his back pocket. He looked at the screen and his eyebrows lifted.

"Wowee, wow. It's your mom. If that's not great timing, I don't know what is." He waved the phone in front of Eva's face.

She opened her mouth, ready to yell the moment he hit the answer button. With one hand, he grabbed her by the neck and drove her against the wall. Her head hit the concrete with such force that it made her vision dance. He pressed the side of his face to hers and spoke into her ear. "Make a noise and I'll crush your windpipe. Fear and respect. Remember that, Eva. I'm the good guy. Right now I'm being patient." He ran his nose through her hair and inhaled before answering the phone.

"Hi, Lori."

Eva faintly heard her mother's voice. Tears burned her eyes as she struggled to breathe against the pressure of Bill's hand.

"No, I don't think you're being ridiculous at all. A mother's instinct is a powerful thing, and you're right to trust it." He paused as Lori said a few more words. "Yes, of course. I have to tie up a few loose ends around here, and then I'll be right over." He hung up the phone and let go of Eva's neck. "Wow. She sounds rattled."

Eva balled her hands into fists. "Don't hurt her."

Bill chuckled sadly. "I won't. Not today."

"I swear to God, if you even touch her I'll—"

"No, no, no, Eva. Fear and respect. Fear me. Respect me. I know you're capable of it. Your father did it very well."

Eva's voice caught in her throat.

"Eva, I'm going to tell you how this is going to go, and I'm honest. You can trust me and what I tell you. I'm going to be there when the police notify your sweet mother that they've found her baby girl's body. Then, I'm going to be there when she has to identify your lifeless corpse. And when she's devastated and needs someone there to wipe away the tears? You got it. I'm her man. I will live your death every day, and it will be my greatest triumph. Fear me and respect me, Eva, for I am always the victor."

She unclenched her fists. His mood swings frightened her more than his threats of violence. Each time she began to relax, he snapped and stripped her of the confidence she'd gained.

"You look hungry, and I can't imagine you ate at that terrible party. You need your strength. I'll be right back with some breakfast."

The blue basement door creaked as he opened it, and he didn't attempt to close it when he left. Eva watched his body disappear up the carpeted stairs. She waited and looked for shadows in the square of sunlight that slipped through the open door.

Certain he was gone, she slid off of the bunk and landed softly on the concrete floor. Her knee was stiff, but she could bear weight on it. She took two steps forward when the shackle around her ankle pulled tight against her skin. She bent over, grabbed the chain with both hands, and pulled hard. It didn't budge. She crouched on her hands and knees and looked under the cot. He'd bolted the chain into the concrete with a fat metal screw. She yanked at the metal again; this time using her body weight and focusing her strength in short bursts. Nothing. The stairs creaked behind her, and she quickly and noiselessly took a seat back on the lumpy bunk.

"Hope you like cereal," he called from the stairs. "Don't really care for it myself. Not much of a gourmand. Everything else that he had up there is rotten. The visitors I have usually don't stay alive very long. So." He dropped a box of Honey Nut Cheerios in her lap. "Here you go." She couldn't make herself look at him. Instead, she stared at the happy, heart healthy Cheerios bee.

"I'm going to go away for a little while. When I leave, are you going to try to escape?"

"No, I promise," she said as she shook her head.

"It's okay if you do, Eva. It's only natural. You can go ahead and try; I won't be angry. I know you'll be good while I'm gone, but you don't have to worry; it won't be for too long. And I'll be sure to give your mom a hug for you." He snaked one arm behind her back and gave her an awkward half hug.

Eva cringed and didn't look up as he walked away.

"And don't think I've forgotten our deal. I gave you something. When I get back, it's your turn."

This time he closed the blue door, and the deadbolt clicked into place.

TWELVE

Schilling pulled off of Cherry Street and into one of the small neighborhoods spider-webbing off of downtown. Beautifully maintained Craftsman homes lined the street and seemed to turn back the clock with their twentieth-century aesthetic.

"I knew this would happen."

"Rookie mistake number twenty," Schilling drawled. "Thinking you're the only one with a theory."

James flushed red. "I'm shocked by how quickly he chose another victim," he admitted.

"We don't know for sure that that's what took place."

"So you don't think there's a possibility that this girl's been abducted and something bad has happened?" The car rolled over a speed bump.

"Of course there's a possibility, and we'll treat this with the utmost urgency. We also have to stay open to other options so we don't get tunnel vision and miss anything. We already know she was at a party. Maybe she left with a guy and is sleeping it off somewhere."

They pulled up to the house. A black, waist-high wrought-iron fence wrapped around the lot's perimeter and held signs letting intruders know the area was under twenty-four-hour monitoring.

Schilling put the car in park and killed the engine. "Sure seems like someone put a lot of work into keeping people out."

"You going back on your previous irresponsible party girl theory?"

"It's still there until it's proven false, but maybe Ms. Kostas has an angry ex we don't know about."

"I'll be sure to ask." James got out of the car and approached the gate.

"Hi, Detectives?" The front door opened and a woman stepped out of the house onto the expansive covered porch. "Sorry." She pointed a remote toward them and the security gate glided open. "I stepped inside to grab more tissues." She wore loose purple yoga pants and a matching cardigan. She wrapped the flowing sweater tightly around her and sat on the edge of a rocking chair.

"No problem at all, ma'am." Schilling led the pair onto the property. "Are you Lori Kostas?"

"Yes, please have a seat." She motioned to two black rocking chairs opposite her.

The gruff, grumbling Schilling dissolved into one of kindness and sympathy. "I'm Detective Schilling. This is my partner, Detective Graham. We understand that your daughter didn't come home last night, and we'd like to ask you a few questions. Is that okay with you, Ms. Kostas?"

"Yes, I want my daughter found. You can ask me

anything." She dabbed at her red, puffy eyes with a tissue.

"When was the last time that you saw your daughter?" Schilling asked.

"The last time I saw Eva, my daughter's name is Eva, was before she left to go to the Ambassador Hotel downtown. She met her friend Bridget there for a Labor Day party."

"And do you know what time she left the house to go to the party?"

She shook her head. "Around ten, maybe. I'm not sure. I was already gone. I had a date. I came home around midnight, and she wasn't here, but that didn't really surprise me. Eva very rarely drinks, so she usually ends up being someone's designated driver." Her hands trembled as she mindlessly smoothed out the edge of her tissue. "She never lets her friends get behind the wheel if they've been drinking. She's a good girl and this isn't like her. I know something's wrong. I can feel it. She hasn't called, or sent me any messages, and she's not answering her phone." Tears leaked down her cheeks.

The wind picked up and blew the Kleenex from her hand. It floated to the ground near James's foot. He picked it up and held it out to her. "Ms. Kostas, did you hear from her at any time while she was out last night?"

"No. I know I should've texted her to check in, but I'm trying to give her space. I want her to feel like an adult even though she still lives at home."

"And you're sure she made it to the Ambassador?" Schilling asked.

"Yes. I talked to Bridget a little while ago. She said that she was there when Eva arrived at the hotel."

James jotted down a few notes before asking another

question. "Can you think of anyone she may have left the party with? A friend or a boyfriend maybe?"

"No, no. Eva is really only close with Bridget. And she's so busy right now, she doesn't have time for a boyfriend. Her father abandoned us. It happened years ago, but after Eva's dad left, she became a lot more shy and reserved. She doesn't trust too many people. I thought that would help keep her safe." She took a deep, shaky breath.

"Eva's father?" Schilling questioned. "Is he the reason for all of the security measures?"

"He managed the security company that installed everything. It was all paid for, and when he left, I didn't see a reason to take any of it down."

"But you're not worried about him coming back or anyone else trying to harm you or Eva?" James asked.

"Oh, no. Eva's dad left a note making it very clear he was finished with the relationship and wouldn't be coming back, and there's no one I can think of who would want to hurt either of us." The pocket of her long cardigan chimed, and she rushed to take out her phone. "It's only Bridget. She's down the street and will be here soon. Hopefully she knows something that will help." She let the phone drop onto her lap.

"We'll be sure to talk to her when she gets here," James said.

"Thank you. I felt foolish for calling the police, but I know deep down there's something wrong. My daughter's in trouble." Lori's face dropped into her hands and her shoulders shook with her sobs.

James left the rocking chair and crouched next to her. "You were right to call us. We'll find your daughter." He placed his hand on her back and patted it gently as it heaved up and down. "I promise we'll find her."

"Graham, looks like there's a visitor." Schilling motioned to the street.

A petite young woman rushed from a white Camaro to the security gate. It beeped as she quickly punched in a code on the keypad. She paused a moment and the gate slid open. Without waiting, she turned sideways and squeezed through the open space between the moving gate and the fence. Her blond ponytail bounced against her neck as she jogged through the yard.

James walked to the front of the porch. "Are you Bridget?"

"Yes, Bridget Falling. Eva's best friend." She took James's place beside Lori.

"Bridget, you didn't have to come over," Lori said weakly.

Bridget smiled affectionately. "I'm always here for you and Eva." She turned back to James. "I want to help. Is there anything you need from me?"

"I do have a few questions. Mind if we talk over by the gate?"

"Not at all."

Schilling heaved himself from the rocking chair and followed.

"Do you know what time Eva arrived at the hotel and where she parked her car?" James asked.

"I know she was late. She got there sometime around eleven or eleven thirty, I think. Sorry, I had a few drinks before she got there so the time frame part is a little blurry. She did have to park a few blocks away though. She can't parallel park. I'm always telling her she needs to learn, but..." Bridget's voice trailed off.

"Do you remember what she was wearing?" Schilling asked.

"I definitely remember that. A green pleated chiffon mini dress with gold Jimmy Choo wedges."

James hesitated a moment before writing down the description, unsure of what a pleated chiffon mini dress looked like. "Did Eva get into any arguments last night or the days leading up to it? Or does she have any enemies that you know of?"

"She doesn't have any enemies. She's way too nice of a person. But something did happen last night between her and Spencer, Spencer Burke."

"Who is Spencer Burke?" Schilling asked.

"A guy from school."

"A boyfriend?"

"I don't think so. And Eva sent me a text that made it sound like it definitely won't be on in the future."

"Do you know what happened?" Schilling prodded.

"No, I don't know exactly what went down. She sent me this text mentioning it, and she didn't sound scared or hurt or anything. But whatever happened made her leave. I feel so guilty. I pretty much pushed her onto him. I swear to God, if he did anything to her—"

"Miss Falling, you don't need to worry about that. We'll handle Spencer."

James continued the questions. "Any idea where he lives or might be staying?"

"He lives in one of the apartments on campus at TU. I've never been there, so I don't know exactly which one."

"I didn't get a chance to ask Ms. Kostas, but do you have

a picture of Eva?"

"Oh yeah, tons. They're all in here." She took her phone out of her pocket. "If one of you will give me your e-mail I can send them to you."

James took a business card from his wallet and handed it to her. "My number is on there and so is my e-mail address. Send them to me, and if you think of anything else, you can text me or give me a call."

"Will do." Her fingers moved quickly as she entered the number into her phone. "Oh, wait." She paused. "There was this one guy who was looking for her, or at least someone with the same name. Blond, tall, super handsome. I think he said his name is Alex. No, Alek. I was with him all last night, but he left this morning in a huge hurry to find her. Whatever he needed her for was pretty important."

"Alek? With a C or a K?"

"No idea. Probably wasn't looking for the same Eva. He might have even been high on something. Was definitely weird. But cute."

James wrote the name on his notepad.

"Thanks for taking the time to answer our questions, Miss Falling. We'll take care of everything from here," said Schilling.

"Anything you need. Just make sure you find her. I don't think Lori could go on if Eva never came back. She's all she has. I don't know what I would do either." Bridget went back to her phone and walked to the porch to sit by Lori.

"I'm going to go radio in the info about this, uh…" Schilling looked back at his notes. "Spencer Burke. You want to go tell Ms. Kostas we're leaving?"

It was the last thing he wanted to do. Her sadness clung

to him. He knew how it felt to have the person closest to you disappear. "Sure, I'll let her know."

Lori rocked in the chair, staring blankly. "Ms. Kostas, we're going to go follow up with a few people. We'll let you know as soon as we find out anything. I've given Bridget my card in case either of you hear from Eva or remember anything that might be able to help us."

"Thank you," she said flatly.

"Detective, I sent you the pictures of Eva," Bridget said quietly. "There were a few of them, so they might take a minute to get to your inbox."

"Thanks. They'll be a big help." He hurried to the car and got in as Schilling finished his call.

"Think it's anything?" James asked.

"Seems fishy, but I can't put my finger on it yet."

"You know what I can't figure out?" James mused. "If Alek spent the night with Bridget, why was he looking for Eva?"

"Could be a different Eva. Or…" Schilling looked past James to Bridget sitting with Lori on the porch, holding one another. "This may be one of those keep your friends close and your enemies closer scenarios. Let's check out Ms. Falling as well."

THIRTEEN

The resonant wriggling in Alek's chest pressed him forward down a bike path bordering a luxurious field. The bright green grass stretched between two sets of matching apartment buildings. Someone had sprayed "University of Tulsa" into the grass in gold, stenciled letters.

A group of shirtless guys threw a ball back and forth at the end of the lawn, while a cluster of girls sat chatting only a few yards away. Alek sized up the situation, deciding the best course of action was to blend in. He peeled off his sweat soaked shirt, threw it over his shoulder, and jogged up to the four women without questioning his game plan.

"Tell me, where is Eva?" he demanded.

The young women paused in their conversation and stared up at him from the shade of their large umbrella. They wore matching blue strapless cotton dresses with three identical triangles embroidered in gold across the chest. Oversized dark sunglasses sat on the tip of each of their noses and their hair was pulled up in perfect ponytails—one blond, one red, one black, and one brown. Except for their hair color, Alek couldn't tell them apart. Alek recognized the letters they wore and felt a surge of confidence. The women would be allies.

"Excuse me?" Brown asked, arching her eyebrows above her sunglasses.

"I do not have time for your pleasantries," Alek said impatiently.

"I haven't seen you on campus before," Red chirped.

"And I think we'd remember someone with your," Blond lifted her sunglasses and scanned his naked torso, "amazing body. We don't get many new athletes around here."

"Our football program is garbage," Black added. "But you didn't hear that from us."

"I am not concerned with your feet, nor am I interested in your balls. This matter is urgent. Where is Eva?" He shifted his weight and stared down at them.

Red's lips twisted into a smile. "You're funny."

"And assertive," Brown added.

"The guys around here can't play sports, can't shoot, can't hunt, and the only time they drink is when there's a sanctioned party. It's like none of them are even real men. But I bet you are," Black said with a giggle.

He glared at the dark shades covering their eyes. "I am weary of this talk. One of you must answer me. Do you know Eva?"

"Oh, look. He's getting angry. His cheeks are even turning red."

"I am not to be mocked. You will not like me when I am angry," Alek rumbled.

"The Hulk!" Red shouted and clapped her hands. "Do

another one. Do another one. I'm great at this game. I don't even ever have to take shots when we play, but I do anyway."

"You turn anything into a drinking game," Brown said.

"It's my hidden talent. It's why all the guys invite me to their parties. I'm super creative about games and stuff."

"Right, I'm sure that's why they're all calling you. Your creativity."

"Call? I don't talk to them on the phone. All they have to do is text me or send me a message on Facebook."

"You're totally one half of what's wrong with our generation, and why my mom says that I'm better off not getting married." Blond pouted.

"Enough!" Alek shouted. "Talking with you is maddening! It's a wonder how this realm has survived! Why anyone would wish to attach themselves to your sex for a lifetime is something I cannot comprehend."

Brown's mouth flopped open, and the other three erupted into giggles.

"Drama. You're definitely majoring in drama, right? No wonder we've never seen you before. We don't get to that side of campus much," Black said.

Blond shrugged. "The gays get all the good ones."

"But you definitely have your character down. Way to commit," Red cheered.

The three guys stopped their game of catch and jogged over. They stood in a circle between Alek and the girls. The largest one spoke first. "Is there a problem over here?"

"This jerk just yelled at us because we didn't tell him where his girlfriend is," Brown said.

"I don't feel like he yelled. He's just passionate," Red said.

Anger bubbled inside of Alek, and his body tensed as

he fought to control the volume of his voice. "Where is Eva? I demand to know."

"Demand?" the bearded guy in the back asked. "Harsh word, isn't it bro?"

"Any other *demands*, brah?" The one in front puffed his chest.

"Jason, relax," Black said calmly. "He's in some kind of theater class, and he's just practicing his role or whatever."

"Drama douche or not, no one speaks to me with that lack of respect," Jason said.

Alek's patience was gone, and he struggled to contain his frustration. "You will give me the information I seek."

"Or what? You gonna recite some Shakespeare fuckin' where art thou bullshit at me? You've got nothin' you roided out motherfucker." Jason spat on the ground between his twitching feet.

"Someone's feeling froggy," Brown mocked.

"Stay out of this, April. Actually, why don't you gather your stuff and all head back to the house? I don't want any of you to have to watch what I might do."

"Don't send them away!" Alek yelled. "They need to tell me where I can find Eva!"

"Dude, you'd better hope she's at the hospital, because that's where you're headed."

Alek paused, looked at the man standing in front of him flexing the muscles in his chest. Alek had seen this before, and he tamped down his excitement but couldn't conceal a smirk. "Are you planning for a battle?"

"Battle? It's gonna be worse than that. I'm gonna fucking murder you."

Alek accepted the challenge and charged at the babbling

mortal. He wrapped his fingers around his throat and held him in the air. The boy's face turned red and his eyes stretched wide. Spit flew out of his mouth as he gurgled apologies. Alek shook him and chuckled as his body danced limply. The girls screamed and ran behind the remaining two young men.

"Your realm is filled with meaningless chatter. My purpose is far greater than yours. You will answer me and be on your way." He let go and Jason flopped to the grass, coughing and gasping for air. "Now, where can I find Eva?"

"Hey, you! Freeze right there!" Two men in black shirts raced across the field in a golf cart.

"It's campo," Blond squealed. "That's a good thing, right? Now they'll arrest him or whatever."

"No, they'll give us all tickets and hold our transcripts," Jason said, his voice scratchy. "Fucking campus police rent-a-cops. Run, but not to the house. If we get another ticket the fraternity will get suspended."

The girls took off with the two guys only paces behind them.

"You're lucky, bro. I was just getting started," Jason shouted as he chased after the group.

The golf cart bounced closer, and Alek followed the mortals' example. He weaved between the campus' many buildings until the whir of the golf cart faded. "What is worth saving in this realm?" he mumbled.

FOURTEEN

Bill was right about the basement. No one heard her in the concrete jail below the house. She stood as close to the blue door as she could get. The tight shackle cut into her ankle as she screamed for help for what felt like hours. No one came. Now, Eva lay on the bunk. Her ankle throbbed. Silence pulsed around her as she stared at the ceiling. Cracks shot through it, and part of her wished the house would come crashing down on top of her. She didn't want to die, but her imagination convinced her that whatever happened next would be worse.

You can't talk your way out of this. That man will kill you. She sat up and looked around the room for any distraction. *Don't think about how. Don't think about how. Don't think about how.*

The metal table, the kind she'd seen in hundreds of CSI reruns, glared at her from the center of the room. Three sets of straps hung lifelessly off of its sides. "Don't think about that. You're going to get out of here before he has a chance to put you on that table. There must be some way."

She climbed off the bunk and onto the floor. "It'll work this time." She grabbed the chain and yanked. "It has to."

Pulling the chain from the wall was hopeless. Her back and arms burned with exhaustion and blisters bubbled to the surface of her hands.

"Why me?" She wrapped her tender hands in the bottom of the baggy shirt. "Why did he choose my family? We've never done anything to anyone. None of this makes sense." She folded her legs under her and gently rocked back and forth.

"Eva!" Bill's muffled voice sang from behind the blue door. "I'm home!"

She scampered onto the bunk and tried to tuck herself away into a happy corner of her mind. The lock slid and the door handle turned. She sipped small shallow breaths and waited for him to enter. The door groaned and he stepped through.

"Are you feeling any better?" His voice asked the question, but his eyes stared at her like lifeless black marbles. "Yes? No?" The creaking blue door closed behind him.

Unsure of the correct response, Eva stayed silent.

"Well, I had a bit of a time over at your mom's." He rubbed his forehead. "The cops had just left."

Having the police involved made Eva feel a little better. At least she knew there were trained people out looking for her.

"Actually, I'm really surprised they were there at all. Normally someone has to be missing for a couple days before they get involved. And right now, no one can be sure if you're missing or just out playing at some guy's house." He paused and let his gaze bore into her. "Your blond friend was there too. What is her name?"

Eva stayed silent, struggling to not tremble. Bill glared at her. "I'm asking you questions, Eva. I don't like the silent treatment. What is her name?"

"Bridget," Eva sputtered.

"Bridget." Bill rolled the name around in his mouth. "She was there, insisting you aren't *that* kind of girl. They really are worried about you." His tongue wriggled out of his mouth and glossed his bottom lip. It looked wet and gray. It slithered back into its dark hole. "Delightful."

Bill sauntered over and sat next to her on the bunk. He pressed his leg against hers, and Eva's teeth chattered wildly in her mouth. "I told them that everything would work out and that I was sure they'd find you very soon, which is true, in a manner of speaking."

He pressed his hand against her leg and moved it up and down her thigh. Every muscle in Eva's body clenched and tears pricked her eyes. The shiny skin stretched so tight over his knuckles that the creases disappeared.

"I didn't, however, bother to correct them when they said they'd find you alive." His hand stopped in the deep crease where her leg met her body. "Why take all the fun out of it? Their disintegrating hope will make your end that much more gratifying."

He lifted his hand from her leg and ran it through her hair. "The buildup to your death is so fulfilling. I could never have imagined it going this well. Especially after last night's mess and me losing my temper earlier. I have to apologize for that, by the way. I don't normally have such a bad temper. I am sorry."

He put his arm around her shoulder and forced her

quaking body against his. "To prove to you that I am truly sorry, I won't make you admit what your family has done. I know that can be rough for some people, and I don't want to put you through that, okay?"

Eva stared at the blue door while he smeared her hair across his face. His breathing deepened and he shakily exhaled. "I feel like I'm going to bust right out of this skin."

She flinched as he surged off of the bunk. "You're a smart girl, Eva. I think by now you've figured out that this isn't really my house, and that I'm not really Bill. Would you like to know who I am?"

"Yes," she whispered.

"Ten years searching. I'd still be searching if not for Bill. Poor, simple William Morgan. I saw him walking through a village with a group of kids, and I could smell your bloodline all over him. Must have gotten it a little wet before his big trip to save the world, if you know what I mean." His eyebrows wiggled up and down. "Wasn't too difficult after that. He was building houses, I offered to help, and he just smiled his broad, dull smile and let me right in.

"Then, I waited. Got to know more about him. He was so eager to share details of his life with anyone who would sit through his boring, self-righteous tales. And I would sit for hours listening to him talk about his road trip to Mexico, his new lover and her daughter, the house he was renovating, and his mindless career. And the whole time, all I could smell was your mother's stench. That's what your family does, Eva. It pollutes everything and everyone it touches. Even poor, stupid Bill. He even gave me his address and asked me to write to him with updates about the village's progress. He made it all too easy, but mortals usually do. The night he was supposed to leave, I helped him pack his car for the journey back to Tulsa, Oklahoma. He hugged me good-bye and thanked me for my hard work. I thanked him by ripping his arms from his body and hacking him to pieces. Then, I littered chunks of him along the drive." He smiled. "Now I've come full circle. It's poetic really. I will avenge so many deaths with yours. Shall we get started?"

"Who are you?" Eva asked.

He gave a sad smile and shook his head. "All that story and I forgot the point of it. No matter. You wouldn't believe me if I told you, but I'll bet you would if I made you."

He took a small key from his pocket and bent down in front of Eva. The thick metal band tugged at her swollen ankle as he fumbled to unlock the restraint. She waited, calming her nerves to plan her timing perfectly. His arrogance clouded his judgment and kept him from using his key to lock the deadbolt when he returned. If she could get to the door, she could get to freedom.

The weight of the shackle released, and it hit the floor with a glassy clink. She coiled her leg and struck out violently. The force of her foot exploded against his right cheekbone, scraped the side of his face, and pounded into his right shoulder. He cried out and fell back. Eva hopped off the bunk and ran. Her fingers grazed the doorknob when Bill launched himself at her. He wrapped his arms around her legs and drove her into the ground. She hit the concrete and bounced.

"Where is the respect, Eva?" He grabbed her arms and pinned them to the floor as he crawled up her body. Eva bucked her hips up and kicked wildly. He lifted his face and stared at her. Yellowish liquid dripped from the thick flap of skin hanging from his cheek.

"Look at what you've done!" His screech made the skin flap dance. Eva yanked one hand free and ripped the vibrating piece from his face. The skin tore away easily and jiggled in her hand like raw chicken fat.

He let go of her other arm and reared back in pain. Inky liquid spurted from the skinless gash. Eva pushed against him, trying to free her legs from underneath his weight. She screamed as she struggled.

"Is this what you want?!" His voice no longer sounded like Bill's. It was the wild growl of a beast. He shoved his fingertips under the lip of remaining flesh and pulled. His body shook violently as he tore the skin from his face. It slurped and popped as mucous flew from his newly birthed head.

"Is this what you want? You want to see me? Do you now believe?"

Terror overtook Eva and she twisted to get free.

His new flesh was slimy, coal black, and his lips were the color of beefy maggots. He threw the skin he'd been wearing and it hit the wall with a wet slap.

"This is who I am! Do you fear me now?!" Warm, fetid spittle flew at her face as his open palm connected with her cheek.

Pain burst through her head and flashes of light erupted in her vision.

FIFTEEN

Printouts of the pictures littered James's desk. Bridget had been true to her word, e-mailing them shortly after they'd met. The best picture, the one he looked at now, circulated the news, social media blasts, and was featured on flyers passed out around the university campus. Eva's bright smile beamed off the page and directly at him.

"Spencer Burke is guilty of being an asshole, but had nothing to do with Eva's disappearance." Schilling startled him. James shuffled the pictures together and shoved them under a nearby file. "Roberts and Sanchez found him hung over at the Ambassador. He admitted to bringing her back to his room, but we have witnesses that say he didn't leave the building all night." Schilling pulled out his chair and sat down with a grunt. "And, from what he said he tried to pull, it wouldn't surprise me if our girl was laying low at a friend's house. I've seen it countless times before. The guy does something awful, and the girl gets to feeling ashamed and embarrassed like it was her fault. Before you know it, she's hid herself away somewhere no one would suspect. Shouldn't be that way, but it is sometimes."

"You're still not convinced that she was abducted?"

"We have no evidence to prove it one way or another. And last time I checked, not letting your mom know where you are wasn't grounds for a manhunt."

Before James had a chance to respond, Officer Winslow approached their desks. "Detectives, got some still shots for you." He took the file from under his arm and waved it in the air. "They're of the missing girl being abducted."

"So she didn't run off?" Schilling questioned.

James felt his stomach drop. He had been working the case like Eva was taken, but he'd still hoped Schilling was right.

"Not unless the definition of running off has changed," Winslow quipped.

"Well, hand them over." Schilling collected the file.

"The camera that caught what happened didn't exactly get the guy's face."

James furrowed his brow. "Was he wearing some kind of mask?"

"No, the guy's face is just missing."

James stared back blankly at Winslow.

"You're going to have to look at the footage. It should be in your inbox by now."

Schilling turned to his computer and clicked his mouse a few times. "Got it right here," he said.

James and Winslow crowded around behind Schilling.

The video played and a grainy black and white image of Eva's car appeared on the screen.

"Camera is on the southwest corner of 1532 South

Cheyenne. They've been having some vandalism issues at this building. When the weekend security guard went in to review the tapes this morning, he found this instead," Winslow informed.

The video continued to play, and James watched a man in jeans and a hooded sweatshirt enter the view of the security camera. The hood hid his face, and he calmly walked to the car and opened the driver's side door. He dug around the front of the car for a few seconds before exiting and climbing into the backseat.

"Skip forward," Winslow instructed.

Schilling put his hand on the mouse. "How far?"

"About an hour."

"Guy waits for her for an hour?" Schilling asked, incredulous. He clicked and the video skipped forward.

"From this we can tell that she didn't lock her doors," Winslow explained. "No cars drive by, no one's walking around, nada. He just lays down in the backseat and waits."

Seconds ticked by before Eva came into frame.

"Why is she running?" Schilling asked.

"My guess is that something spooked her. The guard said that it's pretty dark and empty on that street at night, which is why they have an issue with vandals."

Eva quickly opened the door and got into the driver's seat.

James felt like he was watching a bad horror movie. He wanted so badly to yell at the screen and tell her not to get into the dark car.

A shadowy figure sat up in the back, and Eva sat in the driver's seat screaming. The time stamp revealed that five minutes and twelve seconds passed before her car door flew open. Eva rolled out of the car and came crashing to the ground. She struggled to pull herself up and dart across the street. She was almost to the sidewalk and out of view of the camera when she stumbled and fell. Anxiety filled James as her attacker calmly opened the car door and set his feet on the ground.

"He must not be worried about getting caught. He's taking his time, and, other than the hood, he doesn't seem to be trying to hide his face," Schilling said.

"He doesn't have to. We never see his face." Schilling and James both looked at Winslow in disbelief. "Don't believe me? Just watch."

Eva's hands moved wildly on the pavement as she tried to inch herself forward. The man came up behind her, and Eva stilled and then rolled over onto her back. Schilling paused the image.

"What in the hell." He looked around the keyboard. "Is there a zoom button on this thing? I can't see his face. It's all blurry."

"It doesn't get any clearer than that," Winslow announced.

"That doesn't make any sense," James said.

"Tell me about it. His features stay all wavy like that."

Schilling muttered something about the evils of technology before resuming the video.

The blurry man squatted next to her and grazed his hand across her legs. She kicked and clawed at his face. Watching Eva in the street helpless and alone infuriated James. A few minutes went by before the man offered her his hand and pulled her to her feet. He supported her weight with one arm while bending over and scooping her legs up with the other. Cradling her in his arms, he strolled to the passenger side of the car. Gently, he placed her in the front seat. He lingered inside the car with her before shutting the door. The blurry man then casually walked over to the driver's side door, opened it, and climbed in.

Winslow interrupted the silence. "Something happens in the car because they don't leave for another seven minutes, but you can't tell what from this angle. So that's all she wrote, folks." He handed James the file.

"At least we now know for sure that she was abducted," Schilling offered.

"Yeah, but there's no audio and we can't see his face," James stated.

"The tech team put it through all of their fancy filters. No luck. Sorry, chief." Winslow shrugged and started to walk away. "Oh." He snapped his fingers and turned back to the detectives. "Almost forgot. They found her car parked by TU's performing arts center. There are no cameras covering that parking lot, though. Word is spreading around campus to contact us if anyone saw anything, but nothing so far."

"Next time bring some good news," Schilling said with a grunt.

The file contained several stills from the video. James looked at each of them before handing them off to Schilling.

"He has to be wearing some type of mask or something that's messing with the camera," James said. "Why else would everything in the picture be clear except for his face?"

"Rookie mistake number ten. Getting bogged down in the details. We don't need to see his face."

"You don't think that's important?" James sat back down at his desk.

"This guy gets in her car and waits for an hour. In the

backseat for an entire hour. Even if he was watching her leave to the hotel, he wouldn't know that she was coming back, unless..." Schilling let James fill in the blanks.

And James did. "Unless he knows her."

SIXTEEN

The life ablaze in Alek's chest longed for the Oracle. The supernatural sparks boiled inside of him, pushing him to continue his search. He shook out his shirt and slid the rough fabric over his head. He brushed off the dust and glanced over his shoulder at the sound of fast approaching footsteps.

"Hey, wait there! I need to talk to you for a second." The officer waved; his navy blue uniform was black with sweat.

Alek let out a sigh and turned around. If it came to it, he could subdue this man easily, but fighting drew attention. "What is it you need?"

"Whoa, calm down. Tulsa Police. Just want to ask you a couple questions," he said.

"Apologies, I thought you were a member of the campus police."

"No, I have a real badge." The cop chuckled and tapped the gold star. "A few other officers and I are canvassing the campus. A young woman by the name of Eva Kostas has gone missing. We found her car over in that parking lot." He pointed to the large lot behind him. "Just wondering if you were out last night. Maybe you saw something that might help. It may not have seemed like a big deal when you saw it, but any little detail could end up being important."

"You said her name is Eva?" he asked to clarify, nervous sweat dotting his forehead.

"Yeah, Eva Kostas. You know her?"

"No, I uh, I am simply saddened by the fact that she or anyone may have disappeared," Alek replied. "How long has she been missing?"

"Since around two o'clock this morning. About..." He squinted down at his watch. "Ten hours or so, now. Here's her picture." He handed Alek one of the flyers he clutched in his perspiring hand. "If you see her or hear anything about her, there's a hotline number at the bottom for you to call. This isn't the first student to go missing, so tell your friends to keep their eyes open when they're out at night. You too. We don't know what kind of creep is out there. And pass that around if you get a chance, will you?" he said before waving another pedestrian down and rushing away.

Alek stared at the crinkled white paper. The colorful image stamped on the page didn't match the gloomy heading, MISSING, hung above the vibrant picture in bold black letters damning the beautiful young woman below. She posed with a hand on each hip of her white dress. The fabric seemed brighter than the white of the paper. It highlighted her tan skin and accentuated her curvy silhouette. Dark brown eyes sparkled up at Alek and enhanced her broad smile. Her hair matched the color of her eyes and fell in thick waves around her shoulders.

"Oracle," he whispered, feeling the fire inside of him

pulse with the word. He folded the flyer and put it in his back pocket. "I must find a faster way to travel."

Alek jogged to a rack of banana yellow mopeds lining the building closest to him. Each had the University of Tulsa logo on it with the words Property Of stamped in bold above. A framed note bolted to the building's brick read: Visit the Activities Office with your student ID to checkout a key and helmet for the university scooters. Failure to do so will result in a fine and a hold will be placed on your transcript. This area is being monitored by CCTV.

"It's too bad you put your shirt back on." Red walked her scooter up behind him and giggled.

"You startled me."

"Sorry." She held out her well-manicured hand. "I don't think I actually introduced myself before. I'm Bethany."

He looked at her hand, and then back up at her. "Hello again, Bethany."

"I understand why you wouldn't want to shake my hand." She smiled coyly at him and adjusted the purse strap slung across her body. "I'm not actually friends with Jason, and I think what you did was mad cool."

"I did not frighten you?"

"Oh, no you did. But it's not like you did something a million other people wouldn't have done. It was deserved. He's a total dick. Is there any way you'd do me a favor? I got this automated text saying that I have to come check in with the Activities Office," she explained. "It's a holiday weekend. You'd think they would have better things to do than stalk students about late scooters."

"Quickly, tell me, what is this favor."

"Oh, sorry. Forgot that you're on a manhunt. I just need

you to hold my scooter while I go inside. I don't want to leave it out here. Campo are vultures. If they scan it and find out that it's late, they'll confiscate it and I don't have a car. It should only take a minute, two tops. Do you have time?"

He nodded and grabbed the scooter's handles.

"Awesome." Bethany clapped. "The keys are in there, so if campo comes up, just sit on it and act like it's yours. They won't bother you."

As soon as her red ponytail was out of sight, Alek removed her water bottle and notebook from the front basket and dropped them on the sidewalk. He threw his leg over the moped and sat on its padded seat. The key was already in the ignition, and he knocked the frilly key chains to the side and read the instructions. *Turn key to START.* He rotated the key to the sticker labeled "start." *Be sure RED brake levers are compressed before hitting the GREEN START button. Rotate handle to accelerate. Always watch for pedestrians.* "Simple enough." He did as instructed and the moped sputtered to life. Alek gripped the handles and turned them toward his body. The scooter lurched forward into the row of matching machines. Alek put his feet on the ground and walked backward off the sidewalk and into the street. "Let's try this again." Slowly, he rotated the handle. The engine's hum intensified, and the scooter inched forward. He relaxed and cranked on the handle. Urgency pulsed through his core, and he let it guide him away from campus.

• • •

Schilling sat hunched over his desk munching on a bagel while studying photos and witness statements.

"We finally got something." James handed Schilling a photo and sat on the only corner of the desk not cluttered by paperwork. "They had to blow the image up to twice its normal size, which is why the clarity looks so bad, but we got him."

The black Ford looked like a speckled rock in the low-resolution photo. "That's his car?" Schilling asked, wiping cream cheese from the corners of his mouth.

"Tech guys pulled it from a LARP video some students were shooting. Got our suspect switching cars in the background."

"A LARP video? What in the hell is that?" Schilling scrunched his brow, highlighting the deep creases in his aging face.

"Live Action Role Play. People get in costume and act like characters from games or books," James explained. "The students shooting that video had crescent moon tattoos painted on their faces and were sneaking around campus pretending to be vampires."

"Strange," he mumbled. "Were they able to get the plates off this and run a check for the address?"

"The resolution is too bad to make anything out, but we put an APB out on the car and have uniforms canvassing the area."

"They find anything in Eva's car?"

James shook his head. "I'm waiting to hear more, but they said it was wiped clean."

Schilling mindlessly clicked his pen. "There has to be something connecting the two victims."

"Besides attending the same school, we can't find anything linking them. No classes, friends, or hobbies in common. They're not even the same body type or ethnicity. Whatever he's looking for has a meaning only he knows," James said.

"Shit." Schilling rubbed his eyes. "We're missing something and running out of time. He killed the last victim less than forty-eight hours after abducting her. If we don't find Eva alive before sunup tomorrow, we'll find her dead come nightfall."

SEVENTEEN

He hit her hard. The side of Eva's face pulsed hot with pain. Bright fluorescent light shone in her eyes, making them water. She squinted and tried to lift her hands to clear her vision, but they stayed pinned by her sides. The creature's shadow hung menacingly on the periphery of Eva's eyesight.

"Good. You're awake." A crackling growl hummed from his throat as he spoke.

Eva squirmed against the restraints binding her hands and legs. With each movement, the bands cut into the flesh of her wrists and ankles. Her blood splattered onto the concrete floor in hot, wet drops. The strap across her forehead dug into the skin above her brow and kept her from turning her face away as he approached.

"I...I'm sorry. I won't do it again. Just let me go," she pleaded.

"I think we both know it's too late for that."

Eva closed her eyes tight. He had ripped off his skin, revealing the face of a monster. She didn't want to see what he was, and she couldn't help but start to believe what he said; Bill was gone and something else took his place. Her chest heaved with silent sobs, and her muscles tightened in fearful anticipation.

"Don't struggle." His last word came out as a hiss. *Ssstrugle.*

The squeak of worn wheels got louder as he rolled a tray up next to her. He sat and his putrid stench washed over her. "I don't need to be polite to you anymore. That's refreshing. Do you want to know my true name?" Metal tools clanked together as he shuffled things around on the tray.

Eva kept her eyes closed and made no response.

"Alastor." A cap unscrewed and liquid gurgled. "Have you heard of me? Did your Yiayiá tell you tales of the Great Avenger?" Scissors snipped through thick paper.

Alastor. His words triggered a faint memory. Something her grandmother said when she was a child. She flipped through the moments she shared with her Yiayiá, and an image of her younger self became clear.

"Yiayiá, you have to keep the closet light on. I can't sleep if it's off."

"Why not? You are big girl now. Nothing in closet hurt you."

"What about Alastor? If all the lights are off, he'll come get me when I'm sleeping and put his mark on me."

"Alastor is nasty, evil demon, but he won't get you. Where you hear that?"

"I read it in one of your books. It said that he can grow new skin and look like anyone he wants. If you don't know what he looks like, how do you know he won't come here?"

"He locked away and only back when horrible crime come."

"But what if he gets out?"

"No."

"I'm still scared, Yiayiá."

Yiayiá sat at the edge of the bed and rubbed Eva's forehead. *"A great magic in you. Don't let anyone steal your power. The power make you unique. Now, you sleep."*

Eva's eyes fluttered open. "You were a bogeyman. I thought everything I read and what she said was made up to keep me in line."

Alastor chuckled softly. It sounded wet and raspy. "She didn't. I'm very real."

"She said I didn't have to be afraid. That you were locked away forever."

"You have so much to learn. But you won't be alive to figure it all out."

Cold liquid hit her forearm. He smeared it around and wiped it off with a rough paper towel.

Horrible crime. "You think someone in my family is responsible for a murder? T...That's not even possible."

"Not *a* murder. Your family has been murdering for centuries." He placed paper on her forearm and smoothed it out with a heavy hand. "They've been trying to rid this realm of the powerful beings who keep it in balance. Banishing us to that stinking hole in the Underworld. Calling *us* evil. We had free rein before the Oracle. *Pythia.*" A growl bubbled in his throat as he removed the paper. "Hundreds of years have passed, but her blood still stinks heavy and sweet within her descendants. The stench is so potent it rubs off on those around you. The smell is good on your mom, but on you..." He leaned over her and into her line of sight. Eva suppressed a scream as his nostrils flared with a deep snorting inhale. "On you it's almost pure." He leaned back, and the stool creaked with his shifted weight. "You have the gift of sight, like the Oracle. You're just too stupid to use it."

A faint clicking rose from the ground followed by the sound of swarming bees.

"W…What is that? What are you going to do to me?" Her voice sounded small and broken.

"Leaving my mark." He touched the buzzing tool to her forearm. It felt like shards of glass scraping her flesh.

Eva's chin quivered, and she sucked in air to hold back her tears.

"I learned tattooing from a member of a Mexican cartel. He killed *many* innocent people, so I slaughtered his family. But I'm sure if I ever left anyone alive, they would say tattooing is a vast improvement over my previous method." He patted her forearm with the paper towel. "Using a knife to carve such an intricate design gets messy. And, until they lost enough blood and passed out, the screaming was distracting."

Tears rolled from the corner of her eyes and disappeared into her hairline.

Alastor lifted the tattoo needles from her skin and the buzzing quieted. "Don't cry now, Eva. Save those tears for me. I just have a little left to go. Then you can cry as much as you want. I promise." He leaned into her and traced the path of her tears with his tongue. She flinched against the warm stickiness. "I can't wait to watch you fight for your life." The stink of his mouth lingered after he pulled away.

The vibrant humming of the tattoo gun began again. The pressure it placed on her tendons made her fingers curl in toward her wrist. Her forearm felt like it was being gnawed by fire.

Eva stared at the fluorescent bulb. *No one is coming, Eva. They won't save you in time.* Anxiety filled her body and made her heartbeat quicken. *You're going to die down here.* The realization set in. *In a basement with a monster.* Her heart raced faster, and she sucked in shallow gulps of air. Her chest tightened, and she lay there panting and hopeless.

"That's what I like to see. Panic. And your timing couldn't be more perfect. Just finished." Something heavy clanked against the tray. "Too bad you won't live to see it." He sighed heavily. "Have you ever felt so amazing you wanted to trap the feeling and relive it later? I'm having one of those moments. Luckily, I have your mom as a souvenir."

He laid his head on her chest over her heart and traced her fresh tattoo. The pain overwhelmed her, and she arched her back to try and pull away from the bald, lumpy head resting under her chin.

"It's intoxicating and arousing. Hope Lori is up for a little fun later."

Eva's sob caught in her throat and erupted into a phlegmy cough.

"You're right. Probably couldn't get her to go for it." He lifted his head and rested his chin on her sternum. "But this is going to be even more fun than screwing your mom."

Every syllable he uttered vibrated through his chin and into her chest. She flexed her legs and fought against the restraints.

"I think we've already figured out that's not going to work. Nothing's going to work. It didn't work for the other girl, and it's not going to work for you. She was rehearsal, though. All the others were rehearsal. You're the main event." He traced her windpipe with his thumb and forefinger. "This is going to be so good."

He opened his mouth and bit into the flesh of his left hand. He shook his head side to side, tearing skin from his hand. Warm fluid dripped from the incision and soaked through Eva's shirt. A large flap of skin hung from his mouth, and he spit it off to the side. His sharp teeth tugged at the tips of each of his fingers. Deflated flesh sacks danced like empty socks as he shook his true hand free from its covering. He threw the flesh glove over his shoulder and stretched his newly revealed fingers. His oversized, knobby knuckles popped with use, and his hand looked twice the size it had before.

"I know. I'm bigger on the inside, under the skin. And now I'll be able to feel you struggle. The tension of your muscles as you fight to stay alive." Slimy wet fingers closed around her neck.

She jerked against the straps holding her limbs and head. "No! Please don't! I'll do anything. Just let me go," she wailed.

"Good Eva!" he shouted above her cries. "Scream for me!"

Through her terror, her grandmother's words echoed loud within in her.

"A great magic in you. Don't let anyone steal your power. The power make you unique. Now, you sleep."

She closed her eyes and let the words wash over her.

Don't let anyone steal your power.

She fought against her instincts and quieted her screams. Alastor squeezed her neck and Eva opened her eyes. Tears steadily leaked down her face, and she silently wished for her mom.

"Come on, Eva!" His eyes searched her face. "Fight for your life!"

She refused to let him turn her last moments into those of desperation and fear. Black spots floated into her vision and air whistled as it fought its way into her lungs. She gave in to the consuming pressure on her throat and readied herself for eternal sleep.

Don't let anyone steal your power.

Alastor snarled and squeezed her neck tighter. A sharp crack fractured the still room, and Eva's body relaxed.

EIGHTEEN

Alek hadn't stopped clenching the talisman in his hand since he fled the campus. He used it as a beacon, centering his thoughts, focusing his energies, guiding him to Eva. A craving burned beneath his ribs, beckoning him to follow its frenzied lead. He surrendered to its pull and let it guide him into an approaching neighborhood.

Picturesque landscaping lined the street behind matching mailboxes. Each house looked like a replica of the one before. The otherworldly force inside of him throbbed, and he chased the pulsing lead to a nearby driveway. He leaned the scooter against its kickstand and squinted into the glow of the setting sun.

The mailbox hung open, so full magazines dotted the dead brown lawn. Remnants of rose bushes lined the walkway, and he followed their thorny, dehydrated sticks to the porch. Every step intensified the sizzling force lying in wait within his lungs. He placed an open palm against the door and his chest shuddered. An amber smoke radiated from his fingertips.

"Eva."

He brought his other hand to the door and shoved violently. It shot backward, splintering against the marble floor. He stepped across the threshold, wood snapped beneath his feet. The pungent odor of rotted food hung thick in the air.

"Eva!" he shouted, rapidly dashing from room to room.

He entered the office, and a sharp pain tore through his chest. "Eva!" he roared, ripping empty bookshelves out of the wall. He pulled at the last shelf, but it clung to the wall like skin. Power tightened his muscles as he crushed the wood into shards. The door it concealed swung open, and Alek descended the dark staircase.

"Come on, Eva! Fight for your life!" a voice growled from up ahead.

Alek clenched his jaw and barreled the rest of the way down the stairs. Wood exploded around him as he crashed through the door and into the basement.

"Eva," he snarled at the sight of her still body.

The creature looming over her turned toward him, foam bubbling in the corners of his mouth.

"I'm sorry," he purred. "You just missed her." A smile slashed his shiny black face as he slid off of the table.

"Sacrifice yourself," Alek commanded.

"I see you recognize in me, what I recognize in you." Alastor circled Alek. "We are not of this realm."

"Return to Tartarus in peace."

Alastor cackled. "But I haven't even started carving her body."

Alek charged the creature. Running into him felt like

hitting a boulder, and Alek grunted as he wrapped his arms around Alastor's waist. He picked him up and slammed him onto the concrete floor. Rage fueled each punch, and black blood oozed from Alastor's mouth. It seeped into a widening pool forming on the floor around his head. Alastor clawed at Alek, but the immortal's speed made it hard to get a firm grip. Alastor brought his leg to his chest and thrust it out, hitting Alek in the ribs and launching him backward. Alek smacked the ground and crashed into a metal stool. He scrambled to his feet and grabbed the stool by its legs. Alastor growled wildly behind him, and Alek spun around. The metal collided with Alastor's face and he took a few wobbly steps back. Alek closed the distance and swung his arm wildly, cracking Alastor in the head again. Alastor dropped to his knees and Alek seized the opportunity to rush to Eva's side.

He ripped away the strap holding her head and lifted her chin. He parted her lips and pressed his open mouth to hers. He exhaled deeply, freeing the power caged within him. The magic tingled in his throat as it rushed from him to her. He cupped her face and felt her cheeks grow hot with every breath he offered. The release of power made his body tremble with exhaustion.

Alek heard a hissing behind him. He broke the seal and turned in time to catch Alastor's fist in his face. The force of the punch knocked Alek sideways, and he crashed against the tray of tattoo supplies. A pair of scissors bounced on the ground a few feet from him. He reached for them, but Alastor's foot connected with his stomach before he made contact. Alek's ribs crunched and pain spiraled through his core. His breath caught in his throat, and he pushed the hurt from his mind to crawl toward the scissors. He collapsed onto the concrete as Alastor brought his leg back in preparation for another devastating blow. Alek gathered his remaining strength, rolled to his back, and sat up. He clenched the scissors tight in both hands and lifted the shears above his head. He growled with pain as he plunged the metal into the top of Alastor's thigh. Alastor roared as Alek tore the blades through his muscle and down to the tip of his knee. Alastor's thigh split like meat. Blood rushed to fill the gap between the muscles. Alek pulled the scissors from Alastor's leg and scrambled to his feet. He yanked the blades apart and tightened his grip on each new weapon as he circled the injured creature. Alastor's wails made Alek shudder. The beast crumpled to a heap on the floor. Thick, black blood gushed from the wound, and Alek felt its warm stickiness on his hands.

"I'll climb back out from that hole in the Underworld. And when I do, I'll butcher everyone you love," Alastor hissed between clenched teeth.

Alek crouched on the ground over Alastor and pressed the blades into each side of his neck. "We'll be waiting." He sliced through the thick muscle. Blood spurted from the gashes, and Alek turned his head away from the spray.

Alastor's body twitched and went limp. The basement was silent except for Alek's labored breathing. He gingerly felt his wounds with his hands, testing his body for damage. It was taking him longer than usual to heal, and he needed to get back to Tartarus before his powers drained, leaving him mortal. Alek dropped his improvised weapons and stumbled over to Eva. Before touching her face, he wiped his bloody hands off on his jeans. Again, he tilted her chin up. He brushed her hair back and blew into Eva the fiery power that led him to her. The power that would awaken the blood of the ancient Oracle.

"Eva?" Alek breathed shallowly and stood, studying her face.

Wind blew through the room, and the bulb hanging from the ceiling cast its light in dizzying circles. A cloud of cackling smoke enveloped them, and Alek felt Pythia's presence.

"Pythia!" Alek shouted. "Was I too late?" The Oracle didn't answer. Instead, her laugh grew louder. "Pythia! Answer me!"

A burst of light flashed over Eva and Alek fell backward. The wind and smoke settled, and Eva's body glowed bright amber. The vibrating light traced her perfectly before hovering above her like thousands of golden fireflies. Eva inhaled sharply. The shimmering light rushed back to her body and collided with a clap.

"Eva?" Alek limped to her side.

Her eyes glimmered bright gold; and quiet laughter seeped from her parted lips. "Thank you, young immortal."

"Pythia?" Eva's eyes rolled back in her head, and he studied her chest to make sure it continued to rise and fall.

Gritting his teeth against the searing pain coursing through his ribs, he tore loose Eva's restraints and reached an arm under her neck and another behind her knees. He slowly carried her to the door and stifled a yelp as he ascended the stairs. Alek felt his powers draining, and he fought the urge to flee to Tartarus. He shuffled out the front door and placed Eva on the lawn. Sirens blared as red and blue lights cut through the night, and Alek lifted his arms in surrender.

NINETEEN

Schilling ticked off the facts with his cracked, calloused fingers. "No prints found on the body or at the scene. The scrapings taken from under the deceased's fingernails didn't contain any DNA. We have a video of the perp's face, but it has no identifiable features."

"And we only have a few hours to find Eva alive," James added.

"This is a nightmare."

"I come bearing gifts." Winslow burst into the squad room, unrolled a wad of papers, and then continued. "Two things. First, an update from Oklahoma Highway Patrol. Federales in Mexico reported thirty-seven similar killings throughout the last decade. Here are some pics. More are on their way." He handed James and Schilling each a set of shiny papers.

James shuffled through the pictures. "Each of these bodies has the same tree tattoo as our victim."

"He's been at it for a long time," Schilling said, reviewing the pictures.

"Yeah, and we're going to stop him. What's the second thing?"

"Oh, you guys are going to love me for this one. A patrol officer got a tip about a car matching the Ford's description. A woman called after seeing the report on the news. Her neighbor has the same car, and she said that—"

James and Schilling sprang to their feet.

"Jesus Christ, Winslow," James said, tossing his partner the car keys.

"Send us the address. Incompetent fuckwit," Schilling muttered.

* * *

Schilling collapsed into the car, wheezing from the jog to the parking lot. "Sycamore Heights," he puffed. "Sixty-seven seventeen Fargo Street, Sycamore Heights."

James hit the lights as the engine turned over. "That's only a few miles outside of where he snags them."

Schilling stepped on the gas, and the tires screeched against the pavement.

"Reported burglary in Sycamore Heights neighborhood." The radio crackled to life and James leaned in to turn it up. "Sixty-seven seventeen Fargo Street in Sycamore Heights." The female dispatcher's confident voice filled the car.

"A burglary? What kind of shit is going on at that house?" Schilling blew through a red light and sped onto the highway.

James grabbed the transmitter. "Two king twelve, en route to location. ETA five minutes."

"Seven Lincoln one, copy. I'm coming in from Lynn Lane. Two king twelve, come in from Seventy-First Street," the officer said decisively.

The car lurched onto the exit, and James braced himself against the door. "Two king twelve, copy, coming in from Seventy-First Street. We're going to need backup."

The dispatcher radio crackled, and then went silent. Then a voice, "On a burglary?"

Schilling grabbed the radio from his partner. "All units converge on sixty-seven seventeen Fargo Street. Repeat, all units converge. Suspect may be armed and dangerous."

The dispatcher huffed, but didn't argue. "Male approached the home on a yellow scooter and was seen breaking down the door and entering the location. Be advised, suspect may be on foot."

"Seven Lincoln one in the area. There are two people on the front lawn—one male, one female. Making contact now."

Lights and noises blurred past as Schilling increased their speed.

"Seven Lincoln one, female is unresponsive. We're going to need some help here."

"Seven Lincoln one, copy. Contacting EMSA." The dispatcher was silent for a few moments before coming back on line. "EMSA is on their way to you."

They turned into the neighborhood, and James held his breath.

The car slowed and he launched himself out of the vehicle. "How is she?" he shouted, running to the officers crouched beside the body.

"She's breathing. We're waiting for the ambulance to get here so they can take her to the hospital." The officer stood and met James on the sidewalk. "She's the missing girl, right? I recognized the tattoo."

More cruisers pulled up with their sirens blaring. "Anyone else in the house?" James asked, ignoring the question.

"Guy over there says they're the only ones, but we haven't had a chance to check."

"I want everything taped off. Detective Schilling will lead a couple officers in to clear the place. No one else enters the house without my permission. Got it?"

The officer nodded.

"Your partner talked to the guy?"

The curly haired blond looked beat up and exhausted in the light the officer's partner shone in his face.

"Yeah, says his name is Alek, but he hasn't gotten much else out of him."

"Alek? We have a witness who says that a guy by that name has been looking for Eva since yesterday."

"He didn't say anything about it while I was over there with them."

"Is this his house?" James asked.

"I don't think so."

"Do you know if he's been holding her here?"

"Nope." He shrugged and stuffed his hands into his pockets. "At least, not yet."

"Do you think maybe, just in case this is the guy who's been picking up women and killing them you might want to have your partner do more than shine a light in his face? Maybe even treat him a little like a suspect in a homicide?"

"I'll go see to that, sir." The officer, chastened, drifted over toward Alek.

Schilling walked up to James. "That our suspect?"

"Don't know yet. You going into the house?"

"Yep. You stay out here with Eva in case she wakes up before they get her loaded in the ambulance. I'll let you know what we find."

James walked over and squatted next to Eva as the EMTs checked her vitals.

"How is she?" he asked.

"From what we can tell, she should be okay physically. Bruising already started around her wrists, ankles, forehead, and neck. It'll intensify and be pretty painful. They'll be able to make her more comfortable at the hospital and do a full work-up. It's nothing she won't recover from. This, on the other hand." He turned her left arm so her palm faced up. "It's pretty, but it's also permanent. It'll probably do the most damage."

The tattoo looked like a shadow against the night's black backdrop.

His gaze methodically studied her body. "Any stab wounds or signs of rape?"

"No stab wounds. They'll run a rape kit at the hospital, but there's no obvious sign of sexual trauma."

The EMTs hoisted Eva to a gurney. James followed as they wheeled her the short distance to the driveway.

"Can you stand with her for a second? Some asshole cop blocked our loading doors."

James smirked. "Yeah, I'll wait."

"I mean. Shit. No offense, Detective." They hurried off in search of the owner of the patrol car.

James looked down at Eva. His eyes lingered on her face. "I get to keep my promise and tell your mom we found you." He lightly grazed the back of her hand with his fingertips.

She let out a series of small, dry coughs.

"Hey, can you hear me?"

Her eyelids barely opened.

He spoke softly. "I'm Detective James Graham. Do you know who did this to you?"

"Where's my mom?" Her faint voice barely permeated the noise-filled air.

"She'll meet you at the hospital as soon as they load you into the ambulance. Do you know what happened?"

"I'm so tired."

"You should sleep. The EMTs will be back soon, and before you know it you'll be with your mom at the hospital." James tried to sound upbeat.

"Stay with me. I don't want to be alone."

"Yeah. Sure, I…I'll ride with you. Let me go tell my partner, and I'll be right back." James looked around for Schilling.

"Don't leave." Eva reached out and loosely grabbed his hand. She winced and pulled her arm back beside her.

"Okay. You sleep. I'll just be right over here." He pointed to a spot about two feet away.

A soft smile brightened her face, and she let her eyelids fall shut.

James cupped his hands around his mouth and yelled. "Schilling! Schilling!"

Schilling handed an evidence bag to a member of the Crime Scene Unit and looked around. James waved his arms in the air until he got his attention.

"Graham! I was just going to come find you."

"Eva woke up. She wants me to ride over to the hospital with her. I figured that I'd wait there until her mom arrives."

"There are a few things you should know before you see Ms. Kostas." Schilling positioned himself so his back faced Eva. He leaned into James and lowered his voice. "That's the boyfriend's house."

"I thought she said Eva didn't have a boyfriend."

"Not Eva's, the mom's boyfriend. And there's no body."

"What do you mean?"

"It's clear someone was bleeding pretty heavily in that basement. Enough that they wouldn't have made it out alive. The guy they were talking to is covered in it, and there are pools of it down there. But there's not a body. No drag marks and only one set of footprints leading out."

"That guy you're talking about. The one with Eva when we got here. We need to talk to him."

"And that's the other thing. Thanks to Tulsa's finest, we can't." Schilling threw up his hands. "He's gone."

TWENTY

Fatigue pulsed through Alek and fed the dull ache growing behind his eyes. He lowered his head and pinched the bridge of his nose. The extra power he carried drained him sooner than expected, compromising his ability to heal.

"Hey, you okay?" the officer asked.

"My body hurts and there is a pounding in my head. I think I might be dying."

"Unless you're gushing out blood or unconscious, you're not going to get out of answering a few questions."

Alek squinted at him. "I assure you, this is just as serious. I have to get home."

The officer chuckled. "I would have picked something better than a headache, but nice try. We'll get you looked at by the EMTs when they get here, but you're not going anywhere."

Alek forced himself to stand upright and breathe normally.

"What condition was the victim in when you found her?"

Alek glanced over to where he gently placed Eva. The police cars painted her red and blue with their flashing lights.

"How was she when you found her?" the officer asked again.

Alek turned his attention back to the man in front of him. "She was unresponsive. She must have been knocked out before I arrived."

The officer took a breath to ask his next question but was interrupted by the blaring sirens of the approaching ambulance. "Hey! Over here!" He turned and shouted to the driver.

Alek took a deep, painful breath and gathered the remaining sparks of power firing within him.

"Hurry up, man! We need you over here now!"

With the cop still preoccupied, Alek channeled his energy and launched himself through the house's open front door and down to the basement. The officers looked frozen in place as he maneuvered around them.

His legs wobbled and every nerve in his body vibrated with fatigue. Exhausted, he fell to his knees next to Alastor's dead body. With an open palm on the corpse's chest, he tightly gripped his talisman and whispered shakily, "Bring us home."

The air warmed and shimmered around him. Spikes of heat danced on his skin, and he relaxed into their electric tingle. The floor melted away, and he fell back against the void between realms. Emptiness blazed around him, and he welcomed the peace and stillness it provided.

"Home," he repeated, barely moving his lips.

Every inch of him felt raw, and he pressed his face into the cold floor firming beneath him. Tartarus filled his body with relief and soothed the pain alive in his muscles. He flopped to his back and stared up at the black, craggy ceiling, rejoicing in the power of his realm.

Away from the tension and commotion of the Mortal Realm, he calmed in his home's tranquility and let himself drift to sleep.

When he awoke, Maiden stood above him, stroking his brow. "Son, you've returned. I have never been so worried about you." Maiden looked down at him. "Are you unwell?"

He slowly rose to his feet. "I've never been that close to losing my power before. I felt it draining away, and there was nothing I could do to stop it."

Maiden wrapped her arms around him and pressed her face against his shoulder. "I know. I could feel you growing weak, and I feared you would not make it back to us. I do not know what I would have done if you were without your powers and trapped in the Mortal Realm." Her voice cracked.

"Give him space." Crone shuffled toward them with Mother not far behind. "He has had a great journey."

"He needs to rest and recharge," said Mother.

"I can't. I must go back and be with Eva. She'll be afraid when she wakes up. Someone has to be there to explain what happened."

"She must also regain her strength. She is reentering the Mortal Realm as a great Oracle. She must rest while her body is made new. There is nothing you can do for her now," Mother said.

"How long do I wait? I have to make sure she's well."

The three Furies shared curious glances. "I sense something more than her safety for which you are concerned," Crone said.

"Something more powerful and lasting," Mother added.

"Son, do you love her?" asked Maiden.

"Love her?" Alek shook his head. "I don't even know her."

"Ah, but has the seed been planted?" Crone asked.

"Give it time to grow, my son," Maiden said.

"Maiden, I see our current situation has taught you nothing about young love," Mother said.

Maiden glared at her sister and crossed her arms over her chest.

"I think you are getting ahead of yourselves. She's beautiful, but I don't love her."

"Yet," Maiden encouraged.

"Good," Mother said relieved. "Some were not put in the realms to love. For their purpose is much more grand."

Sadness balled itself in his throat, and he swallowed hard. He didn't love Eva, but when he looked at her, he felt a way he never had before. It left him wanting more. To hear Mother say love may not be in his destiny left part of him feeling deflated. He pushed the thoughts from his mind and concentrated on his present problem.

"What should be done with him?" He pointed to Alastor, a broken heap in the corner.

"I could smell his fetid corpse when you arrived." Crone wrinkled her nose.

"When his spirit entered the Underworld, it shouted curses and promises of vengeance until it reached the cell," Maiden said.

"He said he would return, but he won't be much of a threat without a body."

The women encircled the carcass and Crone spoke.

"If he were to somehow escape again, gaining a new body would be the least of his worries."

"A soul as evil and powerful as Alastor's could overtake a mortal spirit with little trouble," Mother added.

"Then why is he dressed in that skin suit? The other creatures I encountered while training were in hiding and looked as they always had."

"There are many ways a monster hides itself. Spells, potions, possessions, and this." Crone looked disgusted. "My least favorite. The skin suit, as you called it, is a very fitting description."

"It also offered a valuable lesson. Not all of your foes will appear in their true form. You must learn to trust your instincts," Mother said.

"Now, we wait for Tartarus," Maiden said.

"Wait for Tartarus?"

"She may be weak, but Tartarus knows better than to allow such filth to inhabit her outside of the cell," Mother answered.

Faint hissing erupted and Maiden clapped her hands together. "Here it comes," she said gleefully. "Mind your feet."

The hissing grew louder, and Alek shuffled away from the fast approaching noise.

Beetles raced toward the body. In the candlelight, they looked like a shimmering shadow as they gorged themselves on Alastor's flesh.

"Not what I expected," Alek mumbled.

Maiden took Alek by the arm. "We let this mess distract us, but we must show Alek what has happened."

The Furies buzzed with excitement and pulled him along.

Maiden spoke first. "We were gathered in the Hall of Echoes, checking the status of the fast draining pool, when there was a great burst of amber light."

Mother continued, "Clouds of beautiful gold rolled through Tartarus. Their winds knocked us from our feet, and the sound of thunder pummeled our ears. It disappeared as fast as it came, and when Tartarus calmed—"

"The most beautiful gifts were left in its place," Crone finished.

The women parted and Alek peered into the hall. Small pools rippled on the once barren floor.

"I don't believe what I'm seeing," Alek said.

"You must, for it is because of you," Crone said.

"The power you awoke in Eva granted us this gift." Maiden's voice sounded happy and light.

"Tartarus can feel its warriors uniting. Together, you and Eva will heal our realm, our home," Mother said.

"The curse is far from lifting, but this is an extraordinary beginning," Crone said.

Alek walked between the small pools. "It's just as it was in the stories you told."

"Almost," Maiden said. "It is not as magnificent. But it will be fully restored one day."

Like small, rippling mirrors, they each played a moment in time.

"Eva?" He stopped and crouched down to get a better view.

She looked peaceful in the hospital bed. The same serene expression rested on her face as it had when he placed her on the grass. The woman next to Eva held her hand and lovingly patted her head. She turned as a blond young woman rushed into the room, dropping her oversized purse on the floor as she entered.

"Bridget," Alek whispered. "It *was* the same Eva."

She and Eva's mom hugged for a long time. Their bodies shook as tears streamed down their face. A woman in an oversized white coat and sea foam green pants came in followed by a young man in nice jeans and a button-down shirt. Bridget and Eva's mom stood in a huddle with the doctor while the young man went to Eva's side. Alek recognized him as one of the detectives who arrived shortly before he came home. He tightened his jaw at the sight of the detective leaning close to Eva, studying her. The doctor left and the women returned to Eva's bedside. They both looked relieved and smiled as they spoke to the detective. Eva's mom shook his hand and hugged him.

Alek had seen enough. He stood and continued his walk around the pools, trying his best to hide his jealousy from his mothers.

Get it together, Alek. You don't even know her. There is no reason to be jealous. You are an immortal. He is just a cop. Besides, you don't even know her. He ignored the thoughts, and continued on his way back to the entrance of the Hall of Echoes.

"It's amazing, Mothers. I can't wait to see it fully restored." He put his arms around the three of them, and squeezed them tightly.

TWENTY-ONE

Eva blinked the sleep from her eyes and yawned. Her neck was sore, and she turned it to the side in an attempt to get a deep stretch.

"Well, hey there!" Bill said, smiling gaily down at her. "You dozed off for a little bit. Happens sometimes. The whole process can be tiring."

"What are you doing?" she asked sleepily.

"Don't worry, it's almost over," he assured.

"I don't even want to look at it," Lori groaned. "I never should have come with you."

Bill clucked his tongue. "I think it's turning out to be quite the masterpiece."

Eva sat up and looked around. Fogginess draped her thoughts and blurred her surroundings. "Mom, what's going on?"

"Pay no attention to her grogginess. I've seen it hundreds of times. Every morning from first grade on. It'll wear off soon enough."

"Bill, let go of me." She struggled to free her arm from under his grip. He leaned over it, pinning it down with the weight of his body.

"Who's Bill?" Lori asked.

"Must have been someone you were dreaming about. Huh, Eva?" He set down the tattoo gun and peeled off his latex gloves.

"Hey, Alastor." A tall blond appeared. His curly hair hung in his eyes, and he tossed his head back to clear his vision. "There's someone here to see you." He hooked his thumb in the belt loop of his jeans and waited for further instruction.

"Thank you, Alek. Always there when I need you." He pushed the metal tray away and stood. "Eva, remember to keep that clean. You don't want that beautiful artwork getting infected."

"Thanks," she whispered.

"Oh, and Lori, I'll be over in a few hours to get you. I got two tickets to the ballet, but I thought we could get a bite before the show. I'll call you when I'm on my way."

Lori smirked. "Bye, Alastor. Thank you for permanently scarring my daughter." She glanced at her watch. "I've got to get back to the office. Lots of work to do before my date. I can't take you home, but I sent Bridget a text asking her to come get you. She'll be here soon." She kissed the top of Eva's head and disintegrated into a pile of sparkling confetti.

Eva coughed as she breathed in shimmering mom dust.

"Don't worry about the mess. I'll clean it up. It's part of my job," Alek said, pulling a broom out of his pocket.

Eva unbuckled the strap around her wrist and wiggled her fingers. "It's kind of weird around here, isn't it?"

Alek shrugged. "Are you sure you're not just hung over

from the party?"

Eva thought for a moment. "I do feel kind of strange."

He swept a hand through his tangled curls. "It's been a while since he's done a tree design. I think it looks nice."

"Yeah, I like it too." The fresh tattoo looked alive as it danced with the motion of her moving fingers. "I didn't even feel it."

"That's a plus." He chuckled and awkwardly pulled at the pendant hanging around his neck.

"I like your necklace. Is that a crystal?"

The door alarm jingled and cold air blew Bridget into the room. "Let us leave. There is much to learn on your journey home."

"Sorry about her. She likes to make an entrance." Eva picked up her purse and threw the strap over her shoulder.

"I'll see you around." He waved as she rushed to catch up with Bridget.

"I think you can work on being a little less rude, Bridge." Eva closed the car door and fastened her seatbelt. "That guy in there was really nice and majorly cute. You totally acted like he didn't exist."

"You will find him again." She drove the car around the block and parked in front of an open gas pump.

"Yeah, if I ever decide to get another tattoo." Eva gently traced the tree's barren branches. "And I don't know whether or not that'll happen. I can't even remember why I wanted this one."

"To remind you of your strength."

"Hey!" a muffled voice shouted and tapped on the glass. "Want to roll down your window?"

"Sorry." Eva pushed the button, and the window sank

into the car.

"No problem." He winked at her, his hand twirling a crystal pendant. "Just need to know what kind of gas you want. We have green, pink, or gold."

Eva couldn't take her eyes from his fingers caressing the smooth stone. "Your necklace looks so familiar."

Bridget erupted into laughter, and Eva's tattoo prickled with pain. Her throat felt like it caught fire, and she coughed violently. Black seeped from the tree and formed a puddle on the floorboard. Eva kept her feet away from the paint and wrapped her oozing arm in the bottom of her shirt. When she looked up, the gas station had vanished, and her porch appeared in its place.

She rocked in the comfort of the familiar black rocking chair. "My throat hurts. I need a drink." A glass materialized on the table next to her.

"Ask for aid and it will come." Bridget smiled.

Eva and Bridget sat in silence. The sweat from Eva's glass slowly dripped glittery purple onto the stone.

"Who's that?" Eva shaded her eyes from the sun as a van sputtered to a stop in front of her house. The bright decal on its side advertised *Protective Lawn Care*. "When did we hire Alek's Lawn Care?"

The van's door opened, and a tanned man stepped into the sun. He kept his eyes on Eva as he pushed the lawn mower up the driveway.

"Go to him. He is needed to keep you grounded. To keep you safe," Bridget said.

Eva picked up the glass and stepped off the porch. The cut grass felt like spring, cool and moist beneath her feet.

"You were watching me," she said, standing in the

shadow of his strong frame.

"Would you like me to stop?" His eyes studied her face, the plunging neckline of her dress.

"No," she said, offering him the glass.

He gulped big mouthfuls of liquid. Water trickled off his chin and slid down his bare chest.

"You need a towel. Come inside and I'll get one for you." Eva led him through the living room and into the kitchen. She picked up the dishtowel from the counter and dabbed it against his chest. She looked up and met his hazel eyes. "Your pendant. It's beautiful."

He swept the hair from her face and lifted her mouth to his. She kissed him with newly discovered longing, and he returned her desire. Anticipation tangled her thoughts as he brushed the straps of her dress off her shoulders. The soft cotton caressed her back as it floated to the floor. His hand slid from her shoulder and traveled down the deep curve of her back.

He lifted her, placing her gently on the counter. The firm granite cooled the back of her legs.

"You're so soft...so beautiful," he whispered, his breath hot against her neck.

His rough fingers dug into her hips as he pulled her closer to him. His warm mouth explored her breasts, and she bit her lip to keep from crying out. His scent was intoxicating. She drew in a breath and held it, not wanting to let go of the moment. She wanted more of him. Slowly, she forced air out from between pursed lips.

His fingers teased her with unrelenting promises.

"Please, no." He paused, and she pulled him close to her again. "I mean yes."

Her fingers fumbled blindly with his zipper. His heat and hardness pressed against her, and she relaxed her thighs, inviting him in. She arched against him, her legs trembling. Her mouth welcomed his with ravenous exploration.

The room melted around her, and the sound of their bodies filled her ears. She felt free and wild. Her body pulsed with pleasure and she moaned softly. The talisman bounced against his chest as he thrust deeper into her.

"Eva!" Passion flooded his voice. "Eva!"

White light engulfed the room and brought with it a crowing laughter. The space around her emptied, and she stood fully clothed in a box filled with white.

She squinted against the brightness of the room. "Hello?"

A voice rang out. "Have you found him yet?"

"Found who?" Eva shouted back.

"No," the voice replied, sadly, "you haven't. When you find him is when you'll truly awaken."

TWENTY-TWO

"Something is wrong. The Mortal Realm's sun has risen and set three times, yet she remains asleep," Alek said, crouching over one of the newly formed pools in the Hall of Echoes.

"And you have exhausted yourself looking over her. You must rest, and she must do the same," Maiden replied calmly.

"I can't rest now. I have to go to her. I have to make sure nothing more happens to her so she can help me to restore Tartarus."

"Her body is working harder than you or I could ever imagine. Eva is being rebuilt as the new Oracle. Be patient, my son."

"Patience," he grumbled. "Something I possess little of."

Goose bumps appeared on Alek's arms as Maiden lightly traced his back with her fingertips. "As a little boy, anytime you were scared or sad or restless, I would gently scratch your back like this. It used to relax you. Sometimes it would even send you straight to sleep." A smile lightened her voice. "Do you remember?"

"It is something I'll never forget." He arched his back and groaned quietly as he stretched. "It was simpler then."

"How do you mean?"

"The curse. I didn't understand it like I do now. There was no threat of the mortals being overtaken by evil, and Tartarus was only my home. Not a realm I was tasked with restoring."

"Do you blame me?" Maiden asked quietly.

"What reason would I have to do so?"

"The curse would not exist if not for my foolish behavior, and we would not have had to beg Hera for an answer."

"Then I would not be here." He wrapped a comforting arm around her. "Pay no attention to my complaints. I'm just weary of waiting with no way of helping."

They sat in silence for a moment, watching Eva lay motionless in the hospital bed.

"There may be one thing worth attempting," Maiden said. "However, you must not be upset if nothing comes from it."

"Anything will be better than this spectating. What must I do?"

"Your talisman holds a power from this world that you do not carry within yourself," Maiden explained. "It is the reason you are able to travel between realms and speak to us or others when you are in need. Like an invisible bridge binding us together."

"And the longer I'm in another realm, the more I use my abilities, the faster its power drains. Then I have to come here where we both recharge. I know this already," Alek said, barely keeping the frustration from his voice.

"What you do not know is that the same properties that

allow you to contact this realm when you are away, can also be used to reach those who are in a dream state."

"So with this," he pulled the crystal out from under his shirt, "I am allowed entry into people's dreams?"

"Yes and no," Maiden answered. "Dreaming is a gift reserved for mortals. In the past, it was used as a way for them to speak directly with our Gods, Goddesses, and Oracles. They have since lost their way and now see only what they want."

Alek released the talisman. "If Eva is dreaming, will I be able to help her wake?"

Maiden smiled. "Perhaps. However, you must be gentle in your approach. While in them, dreams are very real to mortals. Eva may not know she is asleep. The dream world she has created will be her reality. She must realize on her own that it is not where she belongs and that she has to awaken."

"How do I reach her if I wasn't given the title of a God?"

"You must know that Pythia is watching."

"Yes, she helped me before when I was in the Mortal Realm."

"If given an opportunity, she will assist again and speak to Eva on your behalf. Pythia will not let the new Oracle be lost in the dream world for too long. She will always be there for her." Maiden's smile glowed, and Alek felt a renewed sense of hope.

"Thank you. At least now I will know that I've done everything within my power."

Her skirt brushed against him as she stood, releasing her syrupy citrus scent. "Anything for you, my son." She leaned over and kissed the top of his head before exiting the hall.

"Use Pythia's energy to reach Eva in her dreams. A

simple enough task."

He removed the talisman from around his neck and held it in both hands. He straightened his posture and grounded his legs to the earth beneath them. Alek closed his eyes and caressed the crystal's smooth surface with his thumb. He pictured a smiling Eva, awake and well.

"Pythia, I hope you are listening. I am in need of your help. Again." He inhaled a large cleansing breath and spoke without reservation.

Wind carries the truth.
Seek, listen, know with your soul.
Look within, stay strong.

A tunnel of air encircled him and brought with it the scents of the Furies. Maiden's saccharine aroma returned, filling his nostrils, sharpening Eva's image. Then Mother's gentle lavender vanilla soothed him while Crone's woodsy-sage scent cleansed the worry from his mind.

Your sleep must now end.
Destiny awaits your touch.
Awaken, Eva!

The wind ceased and Alek remained still. "Pythia?" He waited for her unsettling laughter, but only silence hummed against his ears.

Alek put the talisman back around his neck and dipped his fingers into the small pool. Ripples blurred the loop of images playing.

"Please, let my efforts be rewarded," he whispered.

• • •

AMBER SMOKE

"Found who?" Eva spun around. "Where are you?"

"Quiet!" The room flickered a brilliant gold as the bodiless voice punched out the word.

Eva flinched.

"With time, you will learn there is no need to fear me." The woman's voice was smooth and nourishing. "We are of the same cloth. Sewn into the fabric of this world as foretellers of truth and protectors of the weak."

Air blew through the room, carrying with it the invigorating scent of citrus.

"Can you feel him calling to you, pulling you home?"

Eva brushed the twirling hair out of her face. "Who?"

Another gust swept the room, adding hints of vanilla and lavender.

"Your fates are intertwined. You must not deny your warrior's heart."

A third blast of wind encircled Eva with an earthy scent.

"He is the only force great enough to offer protection from the madness that lurks within your new power. Without him, it will steal pieces of your mind until you are scattered and lost like so many of us who came before you."

Eva shouted against the air roaring through the empty room. "You have the wrong person. I don't have any powers."

Laughter trickled through gusts of wind and Eva closed her eyes.

"Open your eyes, new Oracle. Find your warrior. Discover your abilities. Your new life awaits!"

TWENTY-THREE

"Eva, can you hear me? Eva, try to relax. Everything is okay."

"Mom?" Eva croaked.

"She stepped out for just a moment, but she'll be right back. My name is Maya. You're in the hospital. I'm a nurse. Can you open your eyes for me?"

Eva slowly unpinched her eyelids.

"There we go. Now this is going to be a bit bright, so bear with me."

Light from the nurse's small flashlight flooded Eva's vision, taking her back to the white room and the chilling laughter. "I saw that before, that light. It was in my dream."

"Don't try to get up."

"That light," Eva emphasized, "I saw it."

"I'm not surprised. I've been coming in with it and checking on you like clockwork."

Eva groped blindly at the thin, scratchy blanket. "Do you have my glasses?"

"Oh, yes. Here they are." The nurse placed the plastic

frames in her palm.

"Is everything okay? With me, I mean." She looked around, taking inventory of the various beeping machines. "I'm hooked up to a lot of stuff."

"You'll be fine." She typed a few notes on her laptop before continuing. "But we should really get the doctor in here to go over everything." She closed the computer and set it on the counter next to the door. "I'll go see if I can find her. In the meantime, take my advice and try to relax."

"I will." Eva smiled weakly.

"Eva? Oh, thank God!" Lori burst through the door before it closed all the way. "I went to go get some more coffee and..." Her eyes filled with tears. "Oh, it doesn't matter. The only thing that matters is that you're awake. Everything's going to be okay." Exhaustion poured from her voice.

"Why am I here? Was I in an accident?" Eva searched her mom's tired expression for an explanation.

"You don't remember what happened?"

Eva shook her head. The muscles in her neck were sore and tight, and she massaged them with her hand.

Lori opened her mouth to speak, but a hollow knock interrupted her.

"Come in," Eva called instinctually.

The door opened and a tall dark-haired man walked through. His five o'clock shadow enhanced his strong jaw. "Hi, Eva, Ms. Kostas." He nodded in Lori's direction.

"Detective, this is probably not the best time. She just woke up."

"No, it's okay, Mom," Eva said, patting Lori's arm.

He approached the foot of the bed and hesitantly put

a hand on the railing. "I rode in the ambulance with you. You're looking much better. But, I can come back later. I understand if you're not ready to talk yet." His kind smile lifted the corner of his eyes.

"I don't know what it is you want to talk to me about, but I'm good to talk now."

"Eva, this is Detective Graham. He and his partner are the men who've been handling your case. I'll be just outside the door if you need me." Lori walked to James and put a hand on his shoulder. "She doesn't remember anything. Please go easy on her."

Eva waited for the door to close to ask her first question. "Mom said you're handling my case? Did I do something wrong?"

"What's the last thing you remember?"

Eva didn't need time to think. Her actions felt like they'd happened only moments before. "I met Bridget at a party. Why aren't you answering me?"

"You've been unconscious for three days. I need to figure out how much you remember about what actually happened."

"Three days. I've been in here for three days?" Her heart beat wildly in her chest. "Why? What happened?"

"You were abducted after you left the party," he said, matter-of-factly.

Snippets of memories flashed before her eyes. She gulped air and squeezed the bedrails to keep the room from spinning.

"Eva, are you okay?"

"There's someone in the backseat." She closed her eyes against the repeating images and steadied her breathing. Familiar laughter seeped into her ears, and she blocked it out along with the memories of her abduction.

"Yes, he hid there and waited for you to leave the party. I can stop if you need me to."

She relaxed her grip. "No, no it's fine."

"Do you remember anything else?"

She shook her head.

"Is it okay if I show you some pictures?" She nodded and he handed her his phone. "Just scroll to the left. If you see anything that looks familiar, or if it's too much, let me know."

"That's the inside of my car," she said, recognizing the first image.

"Do you see anything missing or out of place."

She studied the picture. "No. It looks the same as it always does." She hesitated before tapping the screen for the next photo, not wanting to trigger another avalanche of memories.

"Is this a picture of Bill?"

"Yes, your mother's boyfriend. No one's seen him since the night we found you."

Scream for me! A wild voice rumbled through her mind, and a shadowed wild-eyed face threatened to break through her hazy recollection. *Scream for me!* The voice echoed.

"It wasn't Bill."

"Do you remember someone else?"

"No, I can't remember who. I just know it wasn't him." Laughter tickled at her throat and spilled out of her lips. "I'm sorry. This isn't funny. I...I don't know where that came from."

"It's okay, Eva. This is stressful. I can't imagine how I would react if I were in your place. No one expects you to handle this a certain way." His tone was soft.

"Thank you."

She held his gaze, and he swiftly darted his eyes. "Just doing my job."

"But really, thank you. Waking up in the hospital. Finding all of this out. I feel like I'm going crazy."

"You're not crazy. Whoever did this, *he's* crazy."

"You said that no one's seen Bill since you found me." She placed the phone face down on her lap. "Where exactly did you find me?"

"Actually, I didn't find you." He left the foot of the bed and circled to the side. He picked up the phone from Eva's lap and skipped ahead a few pictures. "He found you. At least he claimed to."

She took the phone and examined the young man pictured. The familiar, delirious chuckle rippled through her thoughts. *You must not deny your warrior's heart.* Eva covered her eyes with her hand and massaged her temple with her thumb. Laughter shook her torso, and she choked it before it burst out of her mouth.

"I need a break. I'm sorry, Detective."

"Knock, knock." A smiling Bridget opened the door. "Oh, I didn't know anyone was in here with you. I'll come back when you're finished."

"No, Bridge. Don't go," Eva said, relieved by her friend's excellent timing.

"Yes, please stay. We were just finishing up." James took the phone from Eva and stepped away from the bed, allowing Bridget space to squeeze by. "If you remember anything else, your mom knows how to reach me. Thank you for your time." He lingered awkwardly for a moment before leaving.

"Swoon," Bridget said as soon as the door closed. "I'd lie in that hospital bed too if I knew he was going to come check on me." They laughed and she climbed onto the bed and curled up next to Eva. Her bright orange sweats looked out of place against the sterility of the hospital room. "But seriously, Eva. You okay?"

"I'll be a lot better once I get out of this place and have time to process everything. I can't believe what's happening."

Bridget held her hand and Eva leaned against her.

"Your mom's talking to the lab coats out there. They're saying you're some kind of miracle," Bridget said, removing a piece of lint from Eva's gown.

"A miracle?"

"Yep. One of the doctors said that he's never seen anyone heal so quickly. At least that's what they were discussing out there."

Bridget's shoulder shook, and Eva sat up to face her friend.

"I thought you were dead," she sobbed. "I didn't want to say anything to your mom, but I never thought they would find you. I'm so sorry for not believing in you. I'm a horrible person and a horrible friend."

"No you're not. I couldn't have picked a better person to be best friends with." Eva wrapped Bridget in a hug, and they cried together.

"Oh God," Bridget sniffled. "This is not attractive." They let go of each other, and used the rough blanket to wipe their faces. "We can't be all puffy faced. Not with Hot Detective in the building." She smiled.

Lori entered the room with the doctor in tow, and

Bridget hopped off of the bed.

"Welcome back, Eva." The woman looked like every other doctor she'd ever seen: long white coat, light green pants, and a disinterested and almost inconvenienced look on her face. Her rehearsed smile revealed teeth matching the clean white of the walls. "Your mom tells me that you're having a hard time remembering what happened. That's not uncommon after a traumatic experience, but we'll keep an eye on it. Overall, how are you feeling?"

She shrugged. "I'm a little sore, and my muscles are kind of tight. Other than that, I feel fine."

"What about your arm? The tattoo. Any swelling or pain?"

"Tattoo?" Her hand flew to the bandage covering her left forearm. She tore at it until the gauze fell in pieces on the bed. The charcoal tree gleamed in the fluorescent lighting. Her stomach churned and the unsettling laughter invaded her thoughts.

"W…What is this?" Her eyes filled with tears as the voice thundered between her temples.

Fight for your life!

The room spun, then went dark.

TWENTY-FOUR

Eva came to a moment later to the sound of voices and the feel of the doctor's gloved hand against her cheek. The doctor stiffened. "I assumed that you knew about the tattoo."

"Well, she didn't. Not yet," Bridget said defensively. "Thanks for totally fucking up that reveal."

"Dr. Cole, can I talk to you outside for a moment?" Lori left the room without waiting for the doctor's reply.

Bridget flipped her hair and glared at the closing door. "Can you believe that doctor? What a total bitch."

"How did I get this?" Eva stared at her arm, ignoring the snot creeping down her upper lip.

"Don't worry about that. Just put the tape back over it and concentrate on getting your strength back." She collected the chunks of gauze and unsuccessfully tried to reapply them over the tattoo.

"I have my strength back, Bridget. Right now, I need you to answer my question. How did I get this giant tree on my arm?"

Bridget dropped her smile and chewed on the inside of her cheek. "Whoever took you, he did it. But not just to you, to his other victim too."

"There's someone else with this tattoo? Where are they?"

"Dead," Bridget said with a squeak.

"This is too much. I've got to get out of here." The pounding behind her eyes returned as she yanked back the thin blankets. "I can't sit in this bed for another minute."

"Just wait, okay? Here." Bridget picked up Eva's contact case and handed it to her. "Put your contacts in, and I'll freshen up your face with a little makeup and tjuz your awful bedhead. We're in the twenty-first century. You can get that tattoo removed in, like, five seconds. Besides, if you let it get to you, he wins."

"What do I do?" Eva took off her glasses and stuck her contacts in her eyes.

"Let me handle everything. You'll feel so much better after you know you look good. It always works for me. Now hand me those wretched goggles, and I'll put them in my purse."

Laughter flooded Eva's thoughts, and she clenched her fists against the pain that followed. It rocketed through her head, making her stomach turn.

"Oh my God. Eva, your hand," Bridget said, balling up the bed sheet.

Her eyes focused on the tenderness pricking her palm. She relaxed her fist, and shards of thick plastic clattered to the floor.

"My head. It hurts so bad."

"Must be some headache. Open your hand all the way," Bridget instructed, dabbing gently at the cuts. She reached behind the bed and pressed the nurse's call button. "Someone will be here in a few seconds to clean this up and get you some pain meds."

The nurse rushed in the room and to Eva's side. "Looks like you've got a nasty cut there." She snatched gloves out of her pocket and put them on with ease before hunching over to inspect Eva's palm. "It's deep. You might need stitches for these. How did it happen?"

"There was a shooting pain in my head, and I guess I squeezed my glasses really hard."

Bridget handed paper towels to the nurse. "At least you're already in the hospital. This is one of the best places to be if you're going to get hurt."

Maya folded the paper and pressed it hard against Eva's hand. Eva flinched and tried to pull away.

"Sorry, I know it hurts. I'm applying pressure to get the bleeding to slow, and then I'll have the doctor come in and take a look at it." She pulled back the paper towels and the kind expression fell from her face. "What the—"

"What? What is it?" Eva straightened her posture and looked at her hand. Her breath caught in her throat.

"No way," Bridget said, frozen in place.

Raw pink stared at Eva from several deep gashes in her palm. Tan skin rushed together to close the wounds. Panic gripped Eva's body, and she yanked her hand back to her chest.

"I…I think I should call the doctor now," Maya said, backing up slowly.

"Wait, no. I think I'm going to be sick. I need your help." Eva jumped off the bed and pulled the nurse toward the bathroom with her. As they got to the door, Eva shoved the nurse in first and slammed the door behind her, keeping it shut with strength that surprised her. "I'm sorry," Eva called out.

"What the fuck was that?" Bridget shouted.

"Keep your voice down!" Eva hissed. "And help me. I can't hold this door for much longer." Maya pushed against the inside of the door, and Eva's feet slid on the tile floor as she forced her weight against it.

"What do you want me to do?"

"The bed. It has wheels. Push it over here."

Bridget rushed to the bed and pushed it toward Eva. "It's a lot heavier than it looks."

"Just hurry!"

The nurse pounded against the door. Her shouts were muffled behind the thick wood.

Bridget slid the foot of the bed next to the door, and Eva grabbed it. "On three, I pull and you push as hard as you can. Ready?" Bridget nodded and Eva started the countdown. "One, two, three!" Eva pulled hard, and the heavy bed rolled into place in front of the door. "Now lock the wheels on your side." They stomped on the levers and slowly backed away from the bed.

Bridget swept a shaking hand through her hair. "What is going on?"

"I didn't know what else to do. You saw my hand."

"Yeah, since when have you been able to heal yourself?"

"How hell am I supposed to know? I just woke up! I wasn't like this a few days ago." Eva brought her hand closer to her face and rubbed her smooth palm with her fingers.

"And since when do we take hostages?"

"Do you have any idea what they would do to me if we

let her go get the doctor?" Eva glanced at the door. It shook against the nurse's escape attempts.

"Oh my God. Shit, shit, shit, shit, shit," Bridget said, frantically pacing around the room.

"Bridget, you have to calm down. You're not helping."

"Calm down? How the fuck am I supposed to do that after everything that's happened?"

Eva walked to Bridget and held her trembling hands in hers. "We have to get out of here. There's no way we can explain any of this."

Bridget took a deep breath and blew it out slowly. "But what about your headaches and this…" She turned Eva's hand so her palm faced up. "Something crazy is happening. Aren't you worried there's something seriously wrong?"

"We need to go. I need to figure out what's going on with me. I can't do that if I'm locked up in a room, and there's no way they're going to let me leave after they see all this and talk to the nurse."

Bridget thought about it for a moment before speaking. "Fine, but you're not leaving without me."

"Bridge—"

"Don't try to talk me out of it. We've been friends for way too long, and I care about you too much to just abandon you. Besides, I helped you commit what I'm pretty sure is a felony. I'd say we're already in this together."

"You're amazing, Bridge." Eva hugged her tight.

"But first we have to get you out of that open back catastrophe they call a gown." Bridget hurried to the oversized purse she'd dropped by the door. "Sweats or jeans?" She pawed through it before holding up the two options. "Which one do you think Olivia Pope would recommend for fleeing the authorities?"

"Seriously?" Eva asked, yanking off the thin layer shielding her from the cold hospital air.

"Jeans it is." She tossed them to Eva along with a balled up T-shirt. "And I've got shoes in here somewhere." Bridget shuffled through the contents and pulled out a pair of tennis shoes.

Eva scrambled to put the clothes on quickly before rushing to the door. "My mom and the doctor are still talking," she said, peering out the tiny window. "Go along with whatever I say, and we might have a chance at getting out of here."

She casually opened the door and walked into the brightly lit hallway.

"Eva, what are you doing out of bed?" Lori hurried over to them, studying Eva's outfit. "And you changed clothes."

"Yeah, I had to get out of that gown. It made me feel all exposed. Luckily, Bridge brought me something to wear."

Bridget nodded enthusiastically. "Whoever designed hospital clothes should be arrested."

"And where do you think you're going? I thought that nice nurse, Maya, was in there with you."

"She left a few minutes ago. She said she'd be right back, but Bridget has to leave, so I thought I'd walk her to the elevator," Eva lied.

"Are you sure you're okay to walk? You don't want to wait for the nurse to come back and bring you a wheelchair?" The concern in Lori's voice filled Eva with guilt.

"No, I'm okay. It's just down the hall. You can see them from here, and I'll only be gone for a second."

"Okay, well, be careful. The nurses' station isn't far

from the elevator. If you start feeling bad, just let one of them know."

Eva wrapped her mom in a hug and buried her face in her hair. "I love you, Mom. Thanks for everything."

"I love you too," she said, returning her daughter's tight embrace. "The doctor and I are almost done out here. I'll be waiting for you in your room when you come back."

She stifled her tears and forced herself to let go of her mom.

"It was good to see you, Ms. Kostas. I'm so glad Eva is doing so well." Bridget eyes widened, and she giggled nervously.

Eva hooked Bridget's arm with hers, and they rushed toward the elevators. "Don't talk to anyone else. You sound like a crazy person," she whispered.

"I guess I'll have to work on how I act when my best friend wakes up from being unconscious for days with super powers, and we both turn into criminals after locking some innocent and really pretty nurse in a bathroom."

"You have a point." Eva stopped in front of the elevators and pushed the down button. "Tell me when my mom goes into the room, but try not to make it look obvious."

Bridget fluffed her hair and glanced over her shoulder. "She's gone."

The elevator dinged, and they rushed in before the door fully opened. Eva ran the control panel and jammed the close button with her thumb. "Close, close, close," she pleaded aloud.

The doors closed sluggishly, and Eva pushed the button for the first floor before collapsing against the cold metal of the elevator. "Please tell me you have your car."

Bridget groped inside her large bag and retrieved a black key fob. "It's getting reupholstered, so I'm driving a rental."

"Thank God."

The elevator opened, revealing lines of chairs and a set of sliding glass doors to the parking lot.

"I'm parked just a few rows back." Bridget led the way as they hurried through the crowded ER waiting room and into the warm evening. "Where are we going?"

"I don't know. I haven't exactly thought that far ahead." Anxiety twitched in Eva's legs, and she quickened her step. "Know of any good hideouts?"

"My place? You have to sign in in order to see anyone who lives in the building. It's definitely the safest place I know." Bridget held up the key and a nearby car chirped. "This is it," she said, jogging to a white SUV.

"It's huge. You can drive this thing?" Eva asked, hoisting herself up.

Bridget let out a small cackle. "Not well. You better put on your seatbelt."

Bridget carefully maneuvered through the parking lot. Eva buckled up and yelled, "They're going to be out here any minute looking for us. Hurry!"

Bridget pulled up to a light and waited for it to turn green before slamming on the gas. The tires squealed against the pavement, and the car lurched forward onto the main road. "You don't have to tell me twice. Just because I majorly suck at driving this boat doesn't mean I don't know how to drive it fast."

TWENTY-FIVE

Suffocating silence filled the Hall of Echoes as Alek waited for the water to calm. He rose to his feet and paced around the pool. "I have done all that I can," he reminded himself. The ripples stilled and a new image took shape.

"She's awake." His voice dropped to a whisper, and he cleared the small lump from his throat. "Of course she is awake." He squatted by the water and studied the silent stream of pictures. "Mothers! You must see this!"

"Did it work, my son?" Maiden hurried to him and crouched by his side.

"What has happened?" Mother asked.

"Alek was able to reach Eva in the dream world. She is now awake." Maiden pointed to the water.

"Then you must be on your way. The Oracle's safety is as important now as it was before," Crone said.

"The pools have been restored, but we do not know for how long. The curse continues. You must make contact with her. Make her understand what is at stake," Mother said.

"For her realm and ours," Maiden added.

"I am ready." Alek stood and the women covered his talisman with their hands.

"It is up to you, my son. As it always has been." Mother's words followed him as their energy propelled him into the Mortal Realm.

Coughing and pained moans met his ears as the ground hardened below his feet and chairs sprang up around him. Alek appeared to be stuck between a wall and a giant metal box.

"Are you an alien?"

Alek looked around for the small voice. "I do not believe so."

A child poked his head around. Either he or Alek were upside down. "A magician? I had one at my birthday party today, but he hit my dad in the face and called him a cheap asshole." His tongue licked at the blue icing staining his mouth. "Then my mom stopped the party. *And then* we had to get in the car and drive all the way here. I had to eat my cake in the backseat. It got everywhere." He smiled like he'd succeeded in climbing Mount Everest.

"I am sorry to hear about your father and your party. Can you tell me where here is exactly?"

"The hospital. It's where you go when you're sick or hurt, like my dad."

"And where in the hospital are we?"

"I'm in front of the snack machine. You're behind it. Are you sure you're not a magician?"

"Mason, get over here. They're taking your father back now." His mom shuffled over and grabbed his hand. "I'm sorry. It's just been one of those days, you know?" She cast a wary glance at Alek.

"But he's magic. He came out of nowhere." Mason leaned away from his mother as she dragged him past the check-in counter and around the corner. The last Alek heard was the boy's mother reminding him to never talk to strangers, especially weird ones.

Alek pried himself out from behind the machine and set himself on the floor right side up. "The hospital," Alek repeated, looking around for any clue to Eva's whereabouts. "This is much different than what I saw in the pool." He headed to the glass doors and paused when they opened automatically. He held out his hand and felt around the empty space. Convinced it was no trap, he walked out to the parking lot and stared up at the tall building. "How am I to find her?" His fingers fumbled around for his talisman. "Pythia, are you still with me?" Only the whirr of the sliding door answered him. "I should've guessed she would not stay after the Oracle was found."

He took a deep breath and scanned the parking lot. A blond head bobbed between cars. "Bridget?" he said, walking toward the woman.

A car horn blared and came to a screeching halt inches from his leg.

"Get the fuck out of the way!" The driver bolted out of the car and to the passenger door. "We need a doctor! My wife is having a baby!" he yelled.

Alek stepped back as a man in blue scrubs rushed a wheelchair to the car. Both men helped the pregnant woman to the chair and quickly wheeled her through the open doors.

Alek turned back to the parking lot in time to see Bridget hop into the SUV. "Shit!" He kicked the car's fender and it crumpled on impact, leaving a shoe-size impression in the metal. The SUV slowly weaved through the parking lot, and Alek looked back at the damaged car. "I have defeated the driving arcade games," he said, rushing to the open driver's side door. "This will not be much more difficult." He pressed his foot on the brake and turned the key. It came to life with a quiet grumble. He tapped the gas and the car rolled forward. "Indeed, it is exactly like the racing games."

Bridget's SUV idled at a red light, and Alek cut through the parking lot and pulled in line behind her. The light turned green and Bridget's tires squealed against the pavement, leaving him in a cloud of foul fumes. Alek slammed on the gas and turned down the road to follow. The back of the car fishtailed into the neighboring lane, barely missing a passing motorist. Alek yanked at the wheel and regained control of the car. Bridget's SUV slowed, and then abruptly pulled into a parking lot. Brake lights of the car in front of him flashed red, and Alek slammed on his to keep from wrecking. Without pulling over, he put the car in park and ran to the SUV.

• • •

Eva gripped the leather seat as the SUV sped down the road. "Don't do anything that'll get us sent back to the hospital. They've had to find the nurse by now; I'm sure they're looking for us."

"It'll be fine." She tapped the brake and swerved around a turning car. "We'll disappear to my place long enough to come up with a plan for what happens next. And, if we're lucky, no one at the hospital will mention our little lock-up-the-nurse disaster to the cops."

"I wouldn't count on it." Eva yanked on her seatbelt until it was tight across her lap. "When the police talk to you about what happened, I want you to tell them that I made you help me. That I went crazy and forced you to do it against your will."

"No way. I mean, you are crazy, but I'm not going to throw you under the bus like that."

"You have to. You can't tell them the truth."

"I wasn't planning on it. I'm going to use my incredible acting skills and make up something about that nurse going psycho and us having no choice but to trap her in the bathroom. I watch a lot of Netflix crime dramas, and cops are always falling for the I-had-to-do-it-for-my-safety act."

"This is not a show, and I saw you grinning like a fool in front of my mom from one lie. You have absolutely zero acting ability. Even if you did, you'll never be able to explain how my hand healed so fast. No amount of psycho nurse stories will cover what both of you saw."

"Fine. I'll tell them that you forced me to do it. But where does that leave you?"

"I need to find out why all this is happening." She rubbed her hand over her forearm. The stickiness left by the medical tape caught her attention, and she looked down. The harsh black tree coated her arm. Her heartbeat pulsed inside her ears, and she leaned against the door to keep from falling over.

"Eva, you okay?" Bridget's voice echoed far away and tinny. "Hang on, Eva. I'm pulling over."

Laughter swirled around her as a haunting voice charged to the front of her mind. *Have you found him yet?*

The tall, curly haired man pierced her vision, and she pawed around blindly for anything to connect her back to reality. His chiseled features and honey-colored eyes made her stomach flutter as a wave of anxiety passed over her.

Your fates are intertwined. You must not deny your warrior's heart.

Eva bolted upright. "I need to find him."

Bridget leaned over the center console. Concern and fear twisted her delicate features. "Find who? Oh my God, Eva. What the hell? You've been totally out of it for, like, two minutes. I almost said fuck it and just drove you back to the hospital."

"I'm fine now." She pulled her hair into a ponytail and rubbed the back of her neck.

"I don't think you are. You're really scaring me. Maybe we should just go back to the hospital and deal with whatever happens."

"No, please, Bridget. They'll treat me like some kind of freak experiment if we go back."

Bridget sighed and slumped into her seat. "Today was not supposed to end up like this," she said, staring out the window at the passing traffic. "I love you and I'll stick by you, but if you have another…episode I'm taking you back."

"I have to tell you something. I'm going to sound insane, and I won't blame you if you actually think that I am, but I think I know who can help me figure this out."

Bridget moved the gearshift to park and pressed the navigation button on the car's touchscreen. "Let's go there now. Give me his address and I'll put it in. I'm so ready for you to get some answers."

"Well," Eva hesitated. "That's the problem. I don't exactly know who or where he is."

"You're right. You're totally psychotic." Bridget's phone rang, halting their conversation. "Shit. Your mom is calling." She dropped the phone on the center console like it might explode. They both gawked at it as Lori's smiling picture bounced on the screen.

"Don't answer it," Eva whispered.

"Why are you whispering? She can't hear you."

"Then you stop whispering too."

They stared back down at the phone. The buzzing stopped, and the screen darkened.

"Okay, letting it go to voicemail was fine one time, but I can't not answer it forever."

"I know. I know. We'll figure out something to tell her after we come up with a plan."

The phone chimed, and they both jumped.

"Shit, she left a message. Should I check it?"

Eva opened her mouth to speak, but was cut off by loud thuds racing from the back window to Bridget's door. Bridget yelped and ducked down while Eva fumbled with her seatbelt latch.

"Bridget. It's Alek." His voice was quiet, muffled by the window.

"Alek?" Bridget slowly unclenched and rolled down the window. "You scared me to death. What are you doing here?"

"Alek?" Eva's eyes met his. "It's you."

"Wait, you remember him?"

Alek stuck his torso through the open window and leaned across Bridget. "Eva, are you well?" His hazel eyes shined warm and inviting.

"I didn't even know if you were real. How did you find me?"

Bridget put her hands on his chest and pushed him out of the window. "Yeah, how *did* you find us? Shouldn't you be in jail or something? I think the police are after you."

"What is it they suspect me of doing?"

"Besides her, you were the only other person there when the cops raced into the house sirens blazing. So, I'm pretty sure they suspect you of, I don't know, *kidnapping*."

Eva rolled her eyes. "Bridge, he didn't kidnap me."

"I figured that by the oh so calm greeting you gave him." She pressed a button and the door locks released. "Hop in, blondie. There's a lot going down, and we're like sitting ducks out here."

He opened the back door and climbed in behind Bridget. "I have missed something. What role do ducks play in the current situation?"

"I hate to say it, but I think your new boyfriend is kinda slow." She drove the car out of the parking lot and onto the main road.

Alek chuckled. "Your realm has no one with power comparable to mine. My speed can be matched by no man."

Bridget raised an eyebrow and glanced in the rearview mirror. "Have you had anything to drink today? You're sounding pretty crazy, and I know that you can't handle your liquor."

"You two know each other?" Eva asked, surprised.

"We ran into each other at the Ambassador. He was looking for you before I even knew you were missing."

"And I would have reached you sooner had she not attacked me," Alek interjected.

"Attacked you? What happened to mister *no one has as much power as I do*?" Bridget said in her best dumb-jock voice.

"You forced poison down my throat and dragged me into your room."

"*Forced, dragged.* These words are a little harsh, don't you think?"

"Guys! I don't care what happened between the two of you. I want to figure out what's happening to me right now and how you went from being in my head to sitting in the backseat of this car. We can figure everything else out after we're sure no one is chasing us."

"Fine," Bridget mumbled.

"That is why you left the hospital so quickly. Are you in danger?"

Eva turned around in her seat. "How did you know I was at the hospital?"

"On my journey here, I thought only of you. Naturally, that's where I arrived."

"Well, naturally," Bridget mocked. She pulled up to the entrance of the condo complex and passed her key card in front of a large box. The security gate lifted, and she followed the arrows leading up to the parking garage. "So, just to clarify, you've been following her? That's why you were at the Ambassador, that's why you were there when Eva was rescued, and that's why you're here now."

"Precisely," he answered with a smile.

"You can't say precisely like that. Like it's okay that you've been stalking me."

Bridget made a wide turn and swung the SUV into a numbered space. "Yeah, maybe I let you in the car a little too soon."

"I'm only here to keep her safe." He turned back to Eva. "Can you not feel that we're connected?"

She shuddered against the goose bumps rising on her arms "Look, I'm not going to deny that I feel something, but I don't even know you." She opened the door and stepped out of the car.

"But you do feel it?" Alek slid across the backseat.

She slammed the car door and turned, almost running into Alek. His amulet glimmered in the strips of sunlight pouring into the parking garage. "Where did you get that? I swear I've seen it before." Her fingers hovered above the cloudy pink crystal.

"You guys do know that I live upstairs, right?" Bridget asked with her hand on her hip.

"Yeah, sorry, we'll be right there," she said, letting her hand fall.

"Eva, I can help you discover your true self."

"Fine. Then answer my questions."

"As you wish."

"Who are you? Why are you following me?"

"I am Alek, son of the Furies and Immortal Warrior of Tartarus. My only agenda is to unite with you so we may save your realm from evil and mine from destruction."

Eva scoffed and followed Bridget to the elevator. "Okay. You sound bananapants."

"I am offering you the truth," he said, chasing after her. "If not for me, you would be dead. What reason do I have to lie? You saw me in a dream, did you not?"

"He's got a point, Eva," Bridget said, punching the button for the elevator.

"So you believe that he's a warrior from Tartarus and is here so we can join forces and save the world?"

"Well, I'm not sure what Tartarus is, but I do know that

you woke up able to heal like Wolverine, and this guy seems to be closer to having answers than anyone else. I would at least give him a chance and listen to him." The elevator opened and Bridget and Alek stepped in. "You coming?"

TWENTY-SIX

James dropped his phone on his desk and collapsed in to his chair with a sigh. Dull pain pulsed behind his eyes, and he rummaged through his drawers for a bottle of aspirin.

"What'd you find out?" Schilling asked.

"Nothing conclusive." He removed the cap and emptied three pills into his palm. "She says she doesn't remember what happened, but then had a strange reaction when she looked through the pictures. I'm not sure what to make of it." He threw the pills in his mouth and swallowed, ignoring their sour coating.

"You mind sharing a few of those?" Schilling held out his hand, and James tossed him the bottle. "What kind of reaction are you talking about?"

"She recognized Bill and said that he wasn't the one who abducted her. But then she started laughing."

"Laughing? Like something was funny laughing or like she's deranged laughing?"

James shrugged. "I don't know."

Schilling shook out the pills and hammered them with a big gulp of water. "She laugh again when you showed her that picture you took of our suspect?"

"No, she stopped the interview after she saw Alek."

"I can feel you lurking, Winslow," Schilling said without turning to face him.

"You've got that scary Spidey sense, Detective," Winslow said.

Schilling crossed his arms over his chest. "What do you want?"

"Just have some news for you fellas, but don't shoot the messenger." He held up his hands and chuckled.

"Speak, Winslow," James said.

"Got a call from Lori Kostas. She said that Eva's left the hospital, and she can't get ahold of her. She thinks she's with a, uh…" he glanced at the Post-it stuck to his hand. "Bridget Falling. I have her address right here." He handed James the yellow square. "Wants to know if you two will swing by there and get her back to the doctors."

"We're not babysitters," Schilling grunted.

"No, but they also barricaded a nurse in the bathroom before they ran out."

"You're kidding. What for?" James asked.

"Don't know, but you'd think it'd be something pretty bad. I've never heard of someone waking up after being out of it for days to lock someone in a bathroom."

"The nurse, she want to press charges?" Schilling asked.

"Nope. Well, not if you can get Eva back to the hospital. You willing to go give Miss Falling a visit?"

James tried unsuccessfully to stifle a groan.

"I'm taking that as a yes and a thank you." Winslow

flashed a thumbs-up before leaving.

"This may not be a complete fucking waste of time," Schilling muttered, digging car keys out of his desk. "Eva's in on it. I can feel it."

"What, with your Spidey sense?"

Schilling grumbled and headed toward the hall.

"Wait, you really think she had something to do with murdering that TU student? Not to mention strapping herself to a table and having someone tattoo and choke her. She could have died. You think she wanted all of that?" James asked, following his partner to the exit.

"I'm thinking her injuries couldn't have been too bad if she's running away from the hospital."

"No one said she's running."

"There a better reason for her to trap that nurse?"

"You're the one who told me not to jump to conclusions. Something about bending the evidence to fit your assumptions? Rookie mistake number three hundred and eighty? Remember that?"

"I also don't ignore the evidence."

"Neither do I. What we know is that she's confused, scared, and probably disoriented. I can think of several different reasons why she'd feel like she had to get out of the hospital no matter the cost. Fear can make a person do a lot of things."

Schilling stopped in front of the exit doors. "Fine. Let's pick a reason and say she just wanted to stretch her legs. She was almost strangled to death less than four days ago. How bad were they when you saw her?"

"How bad were what?" James asked.

"Her injuries. How bad were they?"

He quietly studied his memory. "I guess I didn't notice anything. Her tattoo was wrapped, but that was it."

"Exactly my point. The Bailey girl was bound, tattooed, strangled, and stabbed from head to toe. But this time the victim wakes up three days later with only a tattoo as evidence of anything happening. They made sure she would only be hurt long enough for us to believe she wasn't involved. They got us chasing our damn tails." He shoved open the door and squinted as he stepped into the sunlight.

"But what reason did Eva have to kill her? We still haven't found a connection between the two of them."

"Maybe they were going after the same guy, or maybe Eva just didn't like the way she was looking at her."

"Yeah, I guess," James said with a sigh.

"Don't you get it? Eva was laughing because of how far off our investigation is. It's been him and her together this whole time, and she thinks it's funny that we've missed it." Schilling pressed the key fob and the car chirped.

"But what about the mom's boyfriend?" James asked, circling to the passenger side. "He just vanished. You think they had reason to get rid of him too?"

"Maybe, if he got in the way. Right now, I don't care about motive. We need to find this Alek No-Last-Name phantom, and I want to bring Eva in and talk to her as a suspect, not a victim."

* * *

"So, what you're telling us is that you're from a mythological place where souls go to spend eternity when they've been damned to hell?" Bridget pressed her code into the keypad attached to her door, and the deadbolt whirred to life. "At least I know you'll be there as eye candy when I'm sent to the fiery pit."

"What I speak of is not myth, nor is it a fiery pit. It's beautiful." Alek's smile faded. "Or it was before the curse."

"Ooh, a curse? Tell me more," Bridget said, holding the door open for them to enter.

"It weakened Tartarus, almost killed it, and made it possible for the creatures it jailed to escape to your realm."

"Don't encourage him, Bridget. At least not until he tells us something useful." Eva sat on the arm of the couch with her back to Alek. "Do you have your phone? We should listen to that message from my mom."

She searched her pockets and emptied her bag on the floor. "Crap, I must have left it in the car." She picked up her keys and paused in the doorway. "Don't say another word until I get back. I want to hear all about this curse." The door closed, and the keypad beeped a few times before locking.

"The curse, that's how Alastor was able to free himself and kill you."

Eva closed her eyes against the rising memories.

"You remember, don't you?" Alek asked, lowering himself onto the velvet armchair across from her. "Now you have proof that what I say is true."

She shrugged. "Maybe I'm starting to believe some things, but you're way off about him killing me. I'm still very much alive."

"Part of you died that night. You did not leave that basement the same woman as when you went down. You now have the power to heal yourself. Who knows what other power you possess? You must feel the changes."

Eva's gaze searched the floor for answers. "I feel *different*. But—"

A buzzer interrupted their conversation.

Alek shot to his feet. Eva rolled her eyes. "Calm down, it's just Bridget."

"Why would Bridget call her own apartment?"

"She's being lazy. She enters a code to get in. She doesn't even have a key." Eva walked toward the door.

"Wait, it's not safe. I will go," he said, jumping in front of her.

"I've got it. It's fine. No one knows we're here. If it's not Bridget it's one of her neighbors' friends. We buzz people in all the time."

"What if it's the people chasing you?"

"No. One. Knows. We're. Here. And I'm not sure if anyone is really chasing me. But if they are, I don't need your help. I'm a big girl." She stepped around him and pressed the video monitor by the door. "Oh my God."

"Who is it?" Alek rushed to her side. His muscles tensed, and Eva's eyes wandered over the tight ripples in his T-shirt.

"It's the cops," she said, pulling her attention back to the door.

"Bridget, you there? It's Detectives Graham and Schilling. We just have a few questions to ask you." James shouted before buzzing again. The loud noise made Eva jump.

"You no longer have to be afraid," Alek spoke quietly and placed his hand on her shoulder.

"It just startled me, that's all."

"I will keep you safe."

Her gaze met his, and she relaxed for the first time since waking up in the hospital. "I know." Her eyes fell to his amulet. The silver-wrapped crystal pulsed a brilliant amber. "That stone. I remember it from in Bill's house, with Alastor. And from my dream."

"It is the last pure piece of my home and how I'm able to travel between realms."

She rubbed her finger against its smooth surface. "Does it always glow like this?"

Alek took his hand off her shoulder and picked up the talisman.

"That's weird. It stopped," Eva said.

Muffled voices caught Eva's attention, and she pressed her face against the door. "Bridget's back."

"What is she saying? What's going on?"

"I don't know. I can't tell," she said, watching the monitor. "Too bad advanced hearing isn't one of your super powers."

The keypad beeped, and Alek pulled her away from the door and into the nearest closet. Fur coats and winter boots filled the cramped space, and Eva pressed her body against Alek's to make enough room to close the door. The crystal flared back to life, and Alek covered the bright beam with his hand.

"Why does it keep doing that?" she whispered.

"I have never witnessed it before. It must have something to do with you. You *are* the Oracle."

"Oracle? What are you talking about?"

"So sorry you waited for so long," Bridget said loudly. "But as you can see, there's no Eva in here."

Footsteps echoed off the hardwood as one of the detectives looked around.

"So Eva didn't come up here with you?" James asked.

"Like I said, she freaked out at the hospital, and I

haven't seen her since she forced me to drop her off at the bus stop."

"And your friend, Alek. Seen him lately?" The detective's country twang made his words rough and choppy.

Bridget chuckled nervously. "I wouldn't really call him a friend. I only talked to him that one time. So, no, I haven't seen him."

"If you do," he continued, "don't approach him. Call us right away. He could be real dangerous."

"Will do." Footsteps returned to the door, and the hinges whined as Bridget opened it. "Thanks for stopping by, Detectives." The door closed, and she let out a big sigh.

Eva pushed open the closet door. "That was way too close."

"You're telling me. I was sure I'd open the door and the two of you would just be standing there out in the open. I'm glad you found someplace to hide."

"And you did a fantastic job lying." Eva tripped over a pair of sparkly Ugg boots and flailed to grab onto anything to keep from falling on her face.

"I got you." Alek's strong arms caught her around the waist. He lifted her to her feet, and she rested in his embrace.

"Thanks." She tucked a few stray hairs behind her ear and smiled up at him.

"Are you two having a moment or no?" Bridget asked.

"No." Eva smoothed out her shirt and backed away. "I, uh, I just—"

"No need to explain. If hunky Hercules wrapped me in those arms we would take a lot longer to get untangled." She smirked.

Alek cleared his throat. "We can no longer stay here. It's

not safe."

"He's right," Eva said, shoving the shoes back in the closet. "We have to go somewhere they won't be looking for us."

"How about our country house? You can stay as long as you need to," Bridget offered.

"Since when do you have a house in the country?"

"Since always. It's north of Mohawk Park, or maybe it's west. I don't know. Either way, we used to go there like every week when we were younger."

"Oh, *that* house. It's definitely still in Tulsa city limits, not the country."

"But it *is* in the absolute middle of nowhere. No one ever goes out there, and it'd be a perfect place to lay low."

"And you are sure the police will not visit there as well?" Alek asked.

"Positive. They'd have to search real hard to even find out about it."

"Bridget, you've already done too much. I can't let you put yourself in another situation that could get you in trouble."

"We have an office full of smarmy lawyers that get paid whether or not they're actually working. Why not give them a little something to do?"

TWENTY-SEVEN

Bridget's country house stood nestled between towering pecan trees on a quiet five acres. She guided the SUV up the long gravel driveway and into the garage. "We may not be in the country country, but it's a good thirty minutes to the nearest Saks," she said, hopping out of the car and leading them into the house.

"I'll take a walk around to be sure this place is safe," Alek said.

"Do whatever you want," Bridget said, dumping her bag on the kitchen counter.

"If you need me, just yell. I will come."

Alek shut the door, and Bridget's eyes immediately darted to Eva. "He's hot, right? You gotta love that macho Superman thing he has going on. And that tight shirt. Sexy, sexy."

Eva shrugged. "I guess. I mean, I have more to think about than how he looks in his clothes."

"*In* his clothes? I was hoping we could find a way to get

him out of them," she snickered.

"Oh, Bridge." Eva rolled her eyes.

"Don't oh Bridge me. I saw how you looked at him when he saved you from face planting on my floor. You were totally loving it."

Eva's cheeks flushed, and she threw a decorative hand towel at Bridget. "Shut up. I was not."

Alek came in through the back door and made sure the deadbolt locked firmly in place behind him. "I believe we are safe."

"Thanks," Eva said, fanning the heat in her cheeks.

Bridget stifled her giggles. "I'm going to go change. Alek, you want to get out of those clothes and into some sweats? Eva and I can dig through my dad's closet. I'm sure we'll find something to dress you up in."

"No," Eva said before Alek had a chance to answer. "I don't think that's necessary."

"Fine. Keep him all to yourself." She flitted down the hall and disappeared into a bedroom.

Eva's shoulders slumped as she stared into the stocked refrigerator.

"Is something troubling you?" Alek leaned against the fridge.

"I just feel so bad about everything. Making Bridget lie to the cops. Lying to my mom. Leaving her with no explanation. This whole thing is a mess." She took a deep breath and held it for a moment. "Sorry," she said, exhaling. "I shouldn't be unloading on you like this. It just feels so natural, you know?"

"We do have air conditioning," Bridget said, returning to the kitchen. She reached around Eva and grabbed a shiny pink can. "Cheers." She popped the top and lifted it in the air.

Eva stared at her blankly.

"What? It's barely even one serving. Can we not just relax for, like, five minutes? No one knows you guys are here, and all of this stress is going to make me break out." She grabbed another can off the shelf before heading to the living room.

"Hey, Bridget, do you have your phone? I want to listen to that message my mom left."

"It's in my bag on the counter." She took a long gulp from the can and collapsed onto the oversized couch. "You guys want to watch a movie?"

Eva grabbed two bottles of water and went to dig through Bridget's purse. "No, I think we're good." She pulled it out of the bag and walked mindlessly to the dining room.

"Your mother left word for you on that phone?" Alek followed her and sat at the head of the table. Eva didn't answer, and he fidgeted slightly. "Would you be more comfortable if I left?"

"You can stay." She pulled out a chair a few seats down and set the phone in front of her on the table. "I don't know whether or not I want to listen to it."

"Knowing what she has to say is better than the constant agony of guessing."

"You're strange sometimes, but you have a point."

"You think I'm strange?"

She pressed the home button, and the phone illuminated. "Yeah, I definitely do."

"Good strange or bad strange?"

A flash of nervousness passed over his face, and she smiled. "I haven't decided yet. I'll let you know after I get all of the answers I'm looking for."

They sat for a moment, and Eva stared at the amulet around his neck. "So your mission is to protect me?"

"It is."

"For how long?"

Alek thought on this. He did not actually know when his mission ended. "When Tartarus is safe, I suppose."

"Is that something that you could bang out in, like, a week? Are we joined at the hip for the next ten years?"

"I am not sure. However long it is, I shall never waver," he reassured. Eva held her breath and tapped the voicemail icon.

"Bridget, it's Lori. If you know where Eva is, please call me. The doctors are saying that her latest round of blood work came back abnormal, and with the headaches and what happened with the nurse…" Lori let out an exhausted sigh. "I'm worried about her. If you're with her, tell her that I'm not mad. I just want to make sure she's safe and okay. Call me. I love you both."

The message ended, and a lump hardened in Eva's throat.

Alek broke the silence. "She sounds frightened."

"And it's my fault," she sniffled.

"Hey! Guys!" Bridget's shouts echoed from the living room. "You really need to come in here and see this."

Eva blinked back her tears and followed Alek to the room. Their pictures, along with Bill's, filled the screen. "Why are we on television?"

"Hang on, I'll turn it up." Bridget reached for the remote and increased the volume.

"In our nightly news top story tonight, police are looking for these three people in connection with the kidnapping and death of Madeline Bailey. As we first reported, Miss Bailey was abducted and her body later found not far from her on-campus home at the University of Tulsa. We'll have more about that developing story later on in the program. If you have any info to the whereabouts of any of these individuals, please contact authorities."

Eva turned away from the TV. "Turn it off. I can't listen to this."

"It's all a big misunderstanding," Bridget said, clicking off the power. "You guys didn't kill that girl."

"Can we not call these authorities and explain what is happening in this realm? Surely they'll want to assist once they learn the truth."

"Before you even finish a sentence, they'll lock you up in some government-funded cell. Even worse, they'll make you put on someone else's underwear." Bridget wrinkled her nose.

"She's right. We can't go to the cops. They obviously think they know what's going on, and they're not going to believe either of us."

Eva flinched as Bridget's phone rang. "It's your work," she said, handing it to Bridget.

"Shit. I totally forgot I was supposed to go in tonight. I can call them back and tell them I'm sick or something."

"No, you can't. You don't want the police or anyone thinking you have something to hide," Eva said.

"Damn. You're right. She circled to the back of the couch and hugged Eva. "I'm so sorry I have to leave. Stay here for as long as you need to. We're going to figure this out. Before you know it, we'll be on a fab vacation somewhere laughing about this whole mess. I love you."

"I love you too." She squeezed her tight before letting go.

"And, Alek, don't go off being stupidly heroic and get yourself caught. I need you to keep her safe. Oh, before I forget." She retrieved a pen and a gum wrapper from her bag and scribbled something down before handing him the paper. "You two be good." She flipped her hair and sauntered down the hall.

Alek glanced at the crinkled strip before folding it and adding to the collection in his back pocket.

Eva sighed and flopped onto the couch. "I can't believe our pictures are on the news. I have no idea how we'll ever sort this out."

"You're the new Oracle. This challenge is nothing compared to the danger we will soon face."

"That's the second time you've called me that. What does it mean?"

"An oracle is someone who—"

"I don't need a mythology lesson," Eva interrupted. "I want to understand what it has to do with me."

"You are a far removed descendant of Pythia, but one of her descendants nevertheless. When I found you lifeless with Alastor, I defeated him and breathed into you new life. That is when the Oracle within you awoke."

Eva shook her head against the memories clouding her thoughts. "But why save me?"

"The curse on my home will not cease until balance is restored and the evil is put back in its place. My flaw is that I cannot stay in this realm for more than a few of your days without losing my abilities and immortality. Because you are the descendant of such a powerful Oracle, and because that blood flows through you so freely, you are the only mortal with enough power to help me."

"What if I don't want to help you? What if I want to go home and try to get back what's left of my normal life?"

"Then Tartarus will break down and die. And all of the wicked souls it holds will claw up and make this realm their own. Alastor and the others hidden here will only be the beginning, and your world will be powerless against them."

"Do you have to make everything so dramatic?" She rested her head on the couch cushion and stared up at the ceiling.

"You must know the truth if you are to make a decision."

Eva closed her eyes and tried to imagine what her Yiayiá would say if she were there. "We can only stay here for a couple days. Do you know where else we can go?"

"I will return to Tartarus in the morning and speak with my mothers. They may be able to offer us assistance." He hopped over the back of the couch and landed next to her.

"Don't take this as me joining forces with you or whatever it is I'm supposed to do. I haven't decided that yet."

"Perhaps you will have better luck in making a decision about our entertainment." He smiled and handed her the remote.

"Have you ever seen *Thor*?" She pulled the blanket off the back of the couch and draped it over their laps. "I think you two have a lot in common." Eva snuggled against him and relaxed into the warm glow of his amulet.

TWENTY-EIGHT

Alek slowly opened his eyes to the shards of sunlight slicing through the blinds. He stifled a yawn and stretched his stiff legs. His arm rested behind Eva's head and buzzed with tingling pinpricks. Carefully, he stood and slid the dead weight out from under her. He shook out his arm until the feeling returned to his fingers.

"Where are you going?" Eva asked, her eyes still closed.

"Home. I will be back shortly. You rest."

"Should I come with you?" She sat up, yawned, and tried to smooth her tangled twists of hair. "What? Why are you smiling at me? Was I drooling?" She wiped at the corners of her mouth.

"No, your hair. It's very reminiscent of Medusa." He chuckled.

"Shut up." She grinned and combed her fingers through the knots. "Your hair doesn't look too great either."

He brushed a hand through his curls and shook his head a few times. "Perfection."

"It's ridiculous how easy it is for guys to get ready." Eva rolled her eyes and fell back against the leather cushion. "If you want me to come with you, it'll only take me a second. I'm sure Bridget has a hat around here, so I won't even have to combat my crazy hair."

"No, stay here. I'll return home alone."

"Oh, okay. Maybe I'll come next time," she said, fidgeting with the blanket.

"Now what is troubling you?" Alek asked, studying her posture.

"Nothing, this still just sounds kind of crazy. If this is some weird prank...I don't know. If I'm really some Oracle and you're, you know, my protector or whatever, I should be able to click my heels and go to Tartarus with you."

"I have only taken carcasses with me on my return. I would not know how to bring a living being."

"Oh, well, that makes sense." Pink flooded her cheeks as she smoothed out the blanket. "How do you get back exactly?"

"My talisman." He rubbed his fingers over its smooth surface. "It holds enough power for my return journey."

"You said that before, but how does it work?"

"Magic," he said, his expression vacant.

She smiled. "Of course. You should ask about that glowing thing it does."

"Yes, the way it lights up when we touch." He tucked the necklace under his shirt and cleared his throat. "I should be going. We don't know when the detectives will return, and we need a plan."

"And while you're gone, I'll go get stuff for our bug-out bag."

"Bug-out bag?" The words felt foreign as he rolled them over his tongue. "You mustn't leave this house." He jogged over to the windows and closed the blinds. "Keep these closed and wait for me until I return."

Eva kicked off the blanket and stood to face him. "I'm not your prisoner. If I want to leave, I will."

Alek furrowed his brow. "I only said to stay to ensure your safety. We don't know who or what is waiting out there."

"Well, maybe I will stay. I could do some research to help me figure out what's going on with you and me and all of this." She waved her hands in the air.

"I will return as quickly as I'm able." He closed his eyes and placed his hand over the covered amulet.

"Wait, you're going now? From right there?" Eva took a few steps back until her calves rested against the couch. "Don't you need more room?"

He sighed and dropped his hand. "What would you have me do?"

"I guess it depends. Are you going to disappear into a puff of smoke, or are you going to spin away like some kind of muscly tornado?"

The corner of his mouth lifted to a half smile. "Would you prefer to watch the muscly tornado?"

"Oh, Lord," Eva mumbled. "I would prefer to not get blown down the hall and destroy Bridget's house."

"That shouldn't be a problem; however, I've never queried those around me as to what happens when I depart."

"You've never done a *query* about it?" she snickered.

"I don't understand what's so humorous."

Eva shook her head. "Just go. I'll jump behind the couch if things get wild."

He again closed his eyes and pressed his fingers into the crystal. *Home.* He focused on the dark pit of Tartarus as the room around him slipped away. *Take me home.*

. . .

Alek relaxed as black earth solidified beneath his feet.

"I can see how much more at ease you are when you return home." Maiden greeted him with a welcoming smile.

"How do you know I don't walk in the Mortal Realm with the same comfort?" he asked, hugging her tightly.

"Have you forgotten the Hall of Echoes has been somewhat restored?"

"You've been keeping watch over me?"

"You *are* my only son. I worry about you."

"If you were watching, then you know there is no reason for your worry. I succeeded in finding the Oracle, and she is safely awaiting my return," he said.

Maiden hooked his arm with hers and they walked slowly together. "And what do you think of the new Oracle?"

Alek shrugged. "I do not yet know how she'll perform in battle. She is headstrong and confusing. I don't believe she fully understands what is at stake for both our realms."

"I am sure she will learn." Maiden lightly patted his bicep. "She is also quite beautiful, would you agree?"

"Beauty does not make a great warrior."

"Women are warriors in many different ways. I have seen the way she looks at you and you at her. Do not deny the battle she is fighting in your heart."

Alek opened his mouth to object, but Maiden held up her hand to stop him. "Halt planning your next move and listen for once. Regardless of what Crone and Mother say, follow what makes you happy. When the curse is broken and you have succeeded, as I now know you will, what will become of your life? You cannot rest in Tartarus for eternity with your mothers as your only companions. Keep your heart and eyes open."

"Sister, to the Hall! Come quickly!" Mother's shouts reverberated off the barren walls.

Alek stretched his stride to keep up with Maiden's quickening pace.

"Alek!" Mother's worried voice hit him as soon as he reached the entrance to the Hall of Echoes. "Thank the Gods you have returned."

"What has happened?" he asked.

"The pools, they are again fading. We will soon be back where we were, defenseless without eyes in the Mortal Realm."

Maiden gasped. "That cannot be."

"I awoke the Oracle and returned Alastor to his prison. How are those deeds not great enough to have lasting effects?" he asked.

"The curse is too powerful," Mother said, crouching beside a small puddle. "Not enough has been done to halt it and permanently outweigh its progress."

He looked past her to Crone's shadowy figure as she circled the shrinking pools. "This battle seems like one I cannot win," he mumbled.

"Nonsense," Crone croaked.

Alek stiffened and walked to the oldest of the sisters.

"My features may be weathered, but my hearing is not." She bent over and blew a strong breath into the pool. Its image blurred as a new one rippled to the surface. "Where is your confidence? You are a warrior, not a boy."

"This curse is never ending," he explained.

"All things end," she scoffed and studied the pool's image before shuffling to the next.

"I must ask for your help, Mothers. Eva is in danger, and I don't know if it's one I can shield her from."

"There is no evil you cannot vanquish," Maiden said.

"True, but this is not an evil. It is a force unique to the Mortal Realm, and it is hunting us both. I need to hide her here until we are sure of our next actions."

"We can offer no more favors or advice," Mother said. "Your sole purpose is to bring about the end of this curse. With the addition of the Oracle's abilities, you have all the tools needed. You must go back and take action."

"Sisters, this should be discussed. If he and the Oracle are truly in danger, sending him away so soon and not offering them sanctuary will not end well," Maiden said.

"There is not time. The curse is overtaking us," Mother retorted.

"And if he or the Oracle is killed there will be nothing standing in the way of its destructive power. All the evil souls held here will rip through to the Mortal Realm and destroy it."

"Look around you, Maiden. Is that not what has already begun?" Mother said.

Maiden turned to Alek and pleaded, "Son, if you expect battle, you must stay longer and make sure your powers are fully recharged."

Alek stared into Maiden's frightened eyes. "Mother is right. I must return to Eva. Valuable seconds are ticking by."

Mother rushed to him. "You are a good man and a better warrior. Now go." She quickly stretched her hand over his talisman. A burst of light flashed from her palm and forced him into the void between realms. "Use your strengths and the Oracle's powers to save us all."

TWENTY-NINE

Restless, Eva walked from room to room admiring the beautiful art and expensive knickknacks neatly arranged throughout the house. She brushed her fingers down the textured wall and smiled at the memories awakening before her. She and Bridget used that hall to practice their *America's Next Top Model* runway skills and to model Mrs. Falling's expensive wardrobe. The pine floorboards creaked under her weight, and she wondered how they were ever able to sneak out successfully.

She leaned against Bridget's doorway and inhaled the light floral scent that always hung in the air. They'd spent countless summer nights searching for a flowery air freshener or candle before Bridget claimed the smell as her natural aroma. Eva entered the room and stepped onto the soft, white rug. She let her bare toes grip the velvety fibers as she rested in the past.

The shrill ring of the phone shredded the memories. She stood still and silent as if the caller would know her whereabouts if she moved. The ringing ended, and she let her shoulders relax away from her ears. She perched on the edge of Bridget's bed and traced the flower pattern on the puffy comforter. She longed for the days of recording fake music videos and lying under the soft blankets gossiping. Those summers felt so far away.

The phone again blared, and Eva followed its ringing into the kitchen. The old landline hung on the wall, and Eva hesitated before picking it up.

"Hello?" she muttered, trying to disguise her voice.

"Finally." Bridget's sigh sounded like a windstorm against the receiver. "I was worried you weren't going to pick up at all. This you-not-having-your-phone thing is a huge pain in my ass."

"It's probably for the best. At least now the cops can't use it to track me. Have you heard anything from them since yesterday?"

"Not a word, thank God. I guess this means I'm in the clear."

"That's great! Finally some good news."

"Right?! See, I told you there's no reason to worry about me."

"I wouldn't go that far, but—"

"Get off my ass!" Eva pulled the phone away from her ear as Bridget shouted and honked. "Sorry, I left work not too long ago, and this guy behind me has been, like, two feet away from my bumper ever since. Crazy bastard!" She cleared her throat before continuing. "What were you saying?"

"So I'm guessing you didn't get fired for going into work late yesterday?"

"They wouldn't dream of firing me. But can you believe

I had to go in and open the store this morning? And when I say morning, I mean early morning. I had to be there before nine. My boss is totally punishing me for coming in late last night. Oh, speaking of late nights, how did yours go?"

"Fine. Alek's gone. He went to Tartarus to see if his mothers will let me stay down there for a little bit." She pinched the phone between her ear and shoulder while she dug through the pantry. "It feels so weird saying that."

"But more importantly, did anything happen?"

She balanced a box of crackers, a can of spray cheese, and a jar of olives as she carefully made her way to the counter. "What do you mean?"

"Do you really need me to spell it out for you?" Bridget asked.

"No." Eva turned on the sink and rinsed her hands. "Where are your knives?"

"Oh my God. You're killing me," Bridget whined.

Eva dried her hands off with a paper towel and rummaged around the silverware drawer.

"Stop fondling the cutlery and answer my question. Did you have sex with the man, Eva?"

"What? No, I didn't even think about it. There's way too much going on. Besides, it's not like that between us."

"Too much going on? We both know if you tell a guy to hurry it can be over in, like, two minutes. Sometimes, you don't even have to say anything, and he's finished before you realize what's happened," she snickered. "And you're hot. So it doesn't really matter whether or not you think there's anything between you, because I'm sure he could make something pop up real quick."

"Sometimes I wonder how we became friends."

"If it wasn't for my expertise, you'd still be a virgin. You totally need me. And I need you to tell me when I'm losing touch with reality."

"Then I think you've lost it on this one," Eva said.

"You don't think he's delicious? You weren't just itching to tear off his shirt and slide your hand down those sweaty abs?"

"Why would he be sweaty?"

"I don't know. Passion and stuff. You're totally missing the point. The idea didn't cross your mind one time?"

Eva sprayed a tube of cheese onto a Ritz.

"That's what I thought," Bridget sang.

"Fine. He's gorgeous, super sweet, has an amazing body, and has that whole I-want-to-protect-you thing going on. I don't know." She sighed.

"If someone that sexy came up to me and said that their whole mission in life was to keep me safe, I'd lose my pants so fast. Guy or girl, doesn't matter. I'm equal opportunity. So just think about it next time the two of you are alone. He's too focused on protecting you to not develop some type of feelings," Bridget said.

"It's all business between us. I'm the oracle, he's the warrior, and there's some serious, possibly life-ending shit going on."

"Okay. I see things just got real. Let me make a suggestion. You need to get out of the house."

"You saw that breaking news story last night. I can't go anywhere. Someone will recognize me, and I'll end up spending the rest of my life in jail."

"I also know that the news jumps to new stories every day, and you're not a celebrity. No one in that bumpkin ass little town is going to recognize you."

"Bridget, we're technically still in Tulsa."

"Yeah, but in the rednecky bumpkiny part. Who knows if they even watch the news?" Bridget said.

"I can't. Alek told me to stay here until he got back. Plus, I'm eating," she said, straining to open the jar of olives.

"Two things. First, since when do you let a man tell you what to do? And second, since when do you let a man tell you what to do?"

"I'm not letting him tell me what to do. It's just because he wants to make sure I stay safe."

"I'll have you back before he even knows you were gone. I promise. It'll be my treat. Pleeeeease?"

"Fine, I'll go. But we're just going to run in and eat really fast and then leave. Deal?"

"Deal. I'll be there in a couple minutes. I'm just down the road."

"How can you be down the road? It takes way more time than that to get here."

"I knew you weren't going to say no, and if you did, I was going follow you around all day until I was able to guilt you into leaving," Bridget said.

"You're awful."

"I know. You have to watch out for me. I can be a real bitch."

Eva shook her head. "I'll be outside. I'll see you in a minute."

She hung the phone up on the receiver and wiped the crumbs off of the counter.

She slipped on a pair of Bridget's Nikes and threw a hoodie over her arm before leaving out the backdoor. The first sign of fall crept into the air and spun its cool breeze around her. She shivered against the sudden cold and stuffed her arms into the baggie sweatshirt.

"Let's go! It's happy hour somewhere!" Bridget leaned out of the window and shouted. The gravel path leading to the house crunched under the heavy wheels of her rental car.

"I'm coming! I'm coming!" Eva jogged to the passenger door and hopped into the lifted SUV.

"The restaurant selection in this part of town is awful. We really only have two choices: pizza or Mexican," Bridget said.

"I'm always up for chips and salsa."

"El Toreador it is!" Bridget cheered, backing down the long driveway and onto the road.

Eva fastened her seatbelt and pushed the baggy sweatshirt sleeves up her arms. "I can't believe it got cold so fast."

"I don't know how you're dealing with any of this. I'd lock myself in my room and be curled up in the fetal position if it were me."

"The thought has crossed my mind," Eva replied, massaging her temples.

"Are you still having those headaches?"

"I'll be fine after I eat something," Eva mumbled.

"Can't you use your insane magical healing power?"

Eva groaned. "I don't know. I don't know how it works."

"Does this mean you're going to live forever? Or at least until someone chops off your head or stabs a wooden stake through your heart?"

"I'm not a zombie or a vampire, Bridget. I'm still me."

"I know. Just throwing out ways to kill the unkillable."

Bridget pulled into the restaurant's parking lot and let the SUV run while she rifled through her purse. "Gloss?" She offered the tube to Eva.

Eva landed on the pavement and shut the heavy door. "Okay, act natural. No one's going to recognize you." She tucked her long hair into the hood and tossed it up over her head. Two cords rested on her chest and she yanked on them, tightening the fabric around her face. Her stomach growled as she walked closer to the scents wafting from the restaurant. "You're just a regular person about to have lunch with a friend. Totally normal."

A car sped into the parking lot and squealed to a stop behind her.

Her hands trembled as she slowly turned to face the car.

The door opened and an officer stepped out slowly. "Eva Kostas?" he shouted.

The navy Charger rhythmically flashed concealed blue and red lights at her, and the officer stood behind the protection of the open door with his hand hovering over his gun.

"Put your hands above your head, turn around, and back up slowly," he instructed.

The thought of running flitted across her mind, but her feet felt glued to the pavement. "W…What's going on?"

"Eva Kostas, turn around and put your hands in the air," the officer repeated.

Slowly, she turned and raised her shaking arms. "I haven't done anything," she said, shocked by the anger penetrating her voice.

"Walk back toward my car," he commanded.

"Whatever you've been told about me isn't true," she

said as she forced her legs to move backward.

"Keep coming back." His footsteps brought his demanding voice closer to her. "Eva Kostas, you're under arrest for the murder of Madeline Bailey. It would be to your benefit if you told me where I can find your partner, Alek." He grabbed her wrist and yanked her arm down.

"Partner? He's not my partner. What are you talking about? I didn't kill anybody and neither did he."

Handcuffs clinked as he unsnapped them from his belt. "You sure you want to protect him? You want to take this all on your own?"

Tires squealed against the pavement, and the clang of crunching metal erupted behind them. And then a voice, familiar, shouting out.

"Run, Eva!"

THIRTY

"Run!" Bridget's screams pierced through the sounds of mangled plastic bouncing around Eva's feet.

Eva didn't hesitate. Adrenaline burst through her body, and her arms felt powerful as she pulled them out of the cop's grip. She charged down the street and took the first turnoff. Her lungs burned as she raced past dilapidated buildings. Weathered siding hung from the houses and cracks separated the pale concrete sidewalk. Sirens whined in the distance, and Eva pushed her aching legs to run faster. She launched herself through unfenced backyards, and into the thick woods. Thin branches whipped her face and clawed at her hoodie. Dead twigs snapped as her feet pounded the uneven terrain. She pumped her arms and raced toward a patch of sunlight. Her body shook, and she slowed her pace to keep from tripping over twisted tree roots marring the earth. She reached the clearing and sank to her knees in the sun's warm glow.

"I can't keep running," she gasped, trying to slow her

thumping heart. Her face stung, and she used her sleeve to wipe away thin lines of blood. Sprinkles of rain dotted the grass, and she lifted her hood to cover her windswept hair. Her breathing calmed, unveiling the intense throbbing between her temples. She rubbed her forehead and rested her face in her palms. "I don't know how to do this by myself." Her tears joined the steady pattering of rain as the sun dipped behind the clouds.

Faint laughter reached her, and she braced herself for the pain she knew would follow.

"You sure there ain't no mountain lions out here, Troy?" The girl's thick Okie accent and intermittent laughter stretched each word.

Eva sat still, her muscles tightening in preparation.

"Shouldn't be," Troy answered. "Not on these trails, but my momma always told me you can't be too sure 'bout nothin'. That's why I'm always carryin'."

The girl's flirty laughter sounded again. "First the zoo, now this walk. Day was almost perfect if not for the rain."

"The day's not over yet. By tonight you'll be back to thinkin' everything's perfect."

The laughter faded as the pair passed.

"The zoo?" Eva's head pounded harder as she stood and examined the trees. "I know where I am."

The pulsing in her head dizzied her vision, and she stumbled onto the trail. The rain beat down more ferociously and soaked her hoodie, making it heavy and cold against her back. The dirt path quickly turned to slick mud, and Eva grabbed on to tree trunks as she hiked up a small incline. Her shoes slipped in the mud, and she dug her toes deep in the slop and kept climbing.

"Almost there. Just a few more yards."

Pain bulleted through her head and wrapped itself around her spine. She lost her hold on the tree and fell face down in the mud. The pain intensified as she dug her hands into the dirt and pulled herself up the slope. "Just a few more yards." She ripped at the rough ferns to get to the top of the hill and crawled a few feet until she no longer felt the rain pelting her back. She put her back against the craggy wall and let her head rest against the rock. She panted and stared up through her tears at the chalky white limestone overhang. Fear rattled inside of her stomach, and she hugged her legs against her chest. "Where are you, Alek?"

·   ·   ·

Bridget drummed her well-manicured fingers against the metal desk as she waited impatiently. They'd removed her cuffs once she arrived at the station, and she studied the raised pink welts circling her wrists.

"Miss Falling," Detective Schilling entered the room first. His thick middle made the buttons on his shirt look like they would pop off at any moment. "I didn't think you would lie to us about seeing your friend."

"And I didn't think I'd be put in handcuffs over a small fender bender." She narrowed her gaze as he sat down across from her.

James scoffed, closing the door behind him. "You rammed your car into a police vehicle, Bridget."

"How was I supposed to know it was a police vehicle? It was just blue. It wasn't even marked."

"I think the officer standing in front of the car

attempting to arrest your friend tipped you off to that fact," Schilling grumbled.

"It was an honest mistake. I dropped my mascara, and my foot slipped. I didn't mean to run into anything," she said innocently.

James dropped a handful of papers on the table and took a seat next to his partner. "Why were you yelling at Eva?"

"I was in shock. I don't remember yelling at anyone."

"You were."

"You're going to have to help me out, Detective. I don't recall."

Schilling sighed, rifled through the papers and held one out at arm's length. "Says here that you repeatedly shouted at the suspect to run." Schilling dropped the paper and stared at Bridget. "And we don't teach our boys to lie."

"Maybe he's confused and is making up a story because he's embarrassed by his terrible police work. Not everyone can be as impressive as you two." She smiled the sincere smile she'd perfected over hundreds of charity events.

"The officer wasn't there for you. He only wanted Eva," James said.

"What's your point?"

"You wouldn't be here right now if not for that little stunt you pulled," Schilling said.

Bridget huffed and crossed her arms over her chest.

"We know it wasn't an accident. Just tell us what happened," James said.

She bit the inside of her cheek. "Someone told me once that sometimes we have to do things that are wrong because we're protecting people who are right." She uncrossed her arms and leaned against the stiff back of the metal chair.

"I may have seen that in an Avengers movie. It's a good line either way."

"So you did it on purpose?" James asked.

Bridget pursed her lips and stayed silent.

"You wanted to give Eva a chance to get away, didn't you?" Schilling asked.

The door opened and a well-dressed man entered. "I see you've already begun," he said, adjusting his glasses.

"Didn't know anyone else was joining us," Schilling said. "Take a seat, Counselor...?"

"O'Brien." The chair squealed as he pulled it across the tiled floor. "I'm here at the request of Miss Falling's parents." He leaned over to Bridget. "You don't need to say anything else."

Schilling glared at the lawyer before continuing. "Did Eva tell you something about what happened to Madeline Bailey? Is that why you wanted to protect her?"

"What, no? She didn't even know her."

"Miss Falling, please. There's nothing you can say to help your friend," O'Brien advised.

"But Eva didn't have anything to do with any of that. And neither did Alek," Bridget blurted.

"I think this interview is over." O'Brien pressed away from the table and stood. "If you're not charging my client with anything else, we'll be on our way. You can address further questions to my office. Let's go, Miss Falling," he said, waiting at the door for Bridget.

"You won't find out who did it. Even if you do, you won't believe it," she whispered before following her lawyer out of the dimly lit room.

Schilling threw down his pen and shoved his chair away

from the table. "Fucking lawyers. Always making my job more difficult. She knows something, but we'll never get it out of her with the army of suits her parents can afford."

"I'm with you on Alek being guilty. But I'm not on board with Eva being a murderer." James's phone beeped with an incoming message. "It's Winslow," he said, reading the text. "An off-duty officer spotted Alek. She's waiting for us there."

THIRTY-ONE

Storm clouds hung low and painted the Oklahoma sky gray. They spit rain from their pregnant puffs and echoed rumbles of thunder. Trapped beneath the thick blanket of clouds, the sun's rays still illuminated the earth with a sickly yellow. Tall grass, golden from months of heat, bowed to each pulse of wind. Lightning dissected the churning skies and slapped the soil with a crack. Sparks flew from the flowerbed lining the front of Bridget's country house.

"Oh, fuck," Alek groaned, rolling up to a seated position. He wiped his dirty hands off on his jeans and removed pieces of mulch from his hair before standing. "I need to get better at that." Hunching his shoulders against sheets of rain, he trudged through the bushes to the front porch. Thunder rumbled as he clenched his fist and pounded on the door. "Eva, I've returned." Water beat steadily on the roof as he waited for a response. "Eva." He knocked again and shuffled to the etched windows bordering the door. The house was dark and still except for the shadows of rain snaking across the floor. He jiggled the handle and thrust his weight against the door. It tore away from its hinges, and fell against the smooth stone entryway.

"The Mortal Realm is in need of better craftsmen," he mumbled, picking up the door and resting it against the wall.

"Eva, are you here?" he shouted. Muddy footprints followed him as he sped through the house, searching each room for the Oracle.

"Why did you not listen?" He balled his fist and thumped it against the kitchen wall. The phone fell off the receiver and drywall dust floated to the floor. Alek picked up the phone. The battery swung from colorful cords, and he stuffed them back into the base. He flipped it over and stared at the call button. "Bridget." He dug in his pocket and pulled out the crinkled gum wrapper she'd given him the night before. He punched in the numbers and held his breath as it rang.

"Who is this and why are you in my house?" she snapped.

"It is where I left Eva," he explained.

"Alek?" she asked, her voice softer.

He nodded before realizing she couldn't see him. "Yes, I'm in need of your assistance."

"I can't really talk to you right now," she whispered.

"I have nowhere else to turn. You're the only one who can help me."

"Hang on." The background noises faded and she spoke again. "Sorry, I got arrested earlier today and now my parents are all over me. I think they would've been happier if I got a DUI."

Alek's stomach dropped. "Did they take Eva?"

"No, I was brilliant and created a diversion so she could get away. But the police are looking for both of you, and

AMBER SMOKE

they're not going to stop anytime soon. They're convinced you guys had something to do with that murdered girl."

"It's not important to me what they think. I must find Eva before they do. Do you know where she is?" He paced around the kitchen, ready to run as soon as he found out her location.

"It's not like we had a what-will-you-do-if-the-cops-try-to-arrest-you conversation before they actually tried to arrest her."

"Think," he barked the command. "You know her better than anyone else. Where would she go?"

"Okay, you don't have to be so rude about it."

The line went silent, and Alek took the phone away from his ear to look at it. "Bridget?"

"I'm thinking, jeeze." She sounded small, and he pressed the phone back to his cheek. "Mohawk Park maybe?"

"Mohawk Park," he repeated. "Are you asking me if she's there?"

"No, that's my best guess. I mean, we weren't too far from it, and we literally went hiking there like every weekend growing up."

Alek ignored her and pressed on to his next question. "How do I get there?"

"Stay on the main road running next to the property, and you'll run right into it in about ten miles."

"Thank you, Bridget."

"And, Alek, when you find her, stay gone."

He dropped the phone on the counter and bolted out the front door.

• • •

Alek barreled down the road. The storm dissipated, leaving gray wisps lazily floating in the sky. Wind dried his shirt and blew the dirt from his body. Visions of a dying Tartarus and a crumbling Mortal Realm fueled his speed and blinded him to the blur of the street.

A force strong and fast clipped his leg and flipped him in the air like a ragdoll. He landed on his feet and quickly crumpled to the pavement. Pain swelled in his leg and tore its claws through his torso. Squealing tires sounded around him as traffic swerved to miss his limp, bleeding body.

A petite woman rushed up and crouched next to him. "Don't move. Don't move," she said, gently patting his trembling shoulder.

"I must get to her." He tried to pull himself up, but his limbs remained motionless and unresponsive.

"Stay still. Don't try to move. It can only make things worse. Can you tell me your name?" Her voice was calm and comforting, unlike the hushed gasps and chatter from the small audience forming around them.

"Alek," he said between wracking coughs.

"Alex, my name is Nina. I'm a police officer. I've called the paramedics. They'll be here very soon," she reassured.

"Police?" he gurgled.

"Save your strength. You're going to be okay."

"I came back too soon," he said, scanning his body internally for any remaining bits of power.

"That doesn't matter now. You'll be fine. Just focus on my voice."

"I need...Mohawk Park," he managed to say between coughs and gasps for air.

"You're only a few feet away from one of the entrances.

Is your family hiking? Or is someone else in there who we should call?" she asked.

He clenched his talisman and felt power surge through his body. "Eva," he whispered.

"Eva, is that the name of your girlfriend? Do you want me to send someone to try and get ahold of her?"

The ambulance whined in the distance, and Alek forced himself to his feet. He cried out as pain stabbed his left leg.

The officer stood and blocked his path to the park. Her neon pink yoga pants had strawberry-colored stains on the knees from his blood. "The ambulance is almost here. You have to lie back down. You've been in a serious accident. You were clipped by a car. I don't even know how you're standing right now."

"Get out of my way," he growled through clenched teeth.

"You look so familiar." Her eyes widened with realization, and she backed up slowly.

Blood streamed down his leg and joined the pool of crimson on the pavement. "Move!" His lip curled with a snarl as he hunched over and pressed his blood-soaked jeans into the wound.

"Think about your next move before you make it. M…my children are in the car," she stammered, glancing back at the small heads curiously gawking out of rolled down windows.

"Then stand down, and I will give them nothing to fuel their nightmares."

She stepped to the side and stared at the concrete. "Just go."

Ambulance sirens blared closer as Alek hobbled into the woods.

The commotion behind him faded as he ventured deeper into the park. Mud camouflaged the paths, and he skated across the ground more than walked. His injured leg stayed useless and bent while the toe of his shoe dug a trench in the sludge.

"Eva!" he shouted, propelling himself forward by lurching from tree to tree. Bloody handprints and syrupy-red splatters added to the trail behind him. "Eva!" he called again. "Can you hear me?"

A calming wave washed over him, dulling his pain, and swirling his vision. "Oracle," he muttered, stretching his arms out in front of him. The trees seemed to lurch back as he reached for them, and he tumbled to his hands and knees. His fingers disappeared in the mud, and he struggled against the suction to free them. His arms shook, and he let his body slump inches from the ground.

"Alek." Her voice fluttered to him like a whisper in a dream.

"I will not die today," he snarled, clenching his fists and pushing off the mushy ground and up to his feet. He bared his teeth and grunted. "I will reach her. Ten more paces."

His hands and feet felt cold and clammy, and the edge of his vision darkened. "Ten more paces," he repeated.

"Eva!" A thin layer of sweat coated his body, and his breathing quickened and became shallower. "Up that hill. Only ten more paces."

His foot slipped in the sludge, and he collapsed to his back on the ground. His body felt tired and empty. He stared at the sky as he let himself sink into the mud.

"Oracle, where are you?"

THIRTY-TWO

Eva's headache lifted with the rain. The excruciating pain vanished and left in its place panic and fear. Scared of anyone who might see her, she didn't dare leave the safety of the small cave. Instead, she focused on meaningless tasks to keep from shattering into a million frightened, blubbering pieces. She dug at drying layers of muck to uncover her pants and shoes. Her body ached, and her hands felt raw and tight. They shook with fatigue and pain as she plucked thorns from her fingers and palms.

"I should have never left the house. Why did I think they wouldn't find me?" Eva rested her head on her knees and rocked back and forth. She sniffled and wiped her nose on her damp, dirty sweat pants.

"Eva." Her ears perked and she stared out the den's wide opening. Her ragged breathing and the soft patter of water echoed around her. She straightened and crawled to the mouth of the cave. Her hands and knees throbbed as she stretched her neck to listen. "Eva. Can you hear me?"

"Alek?" She launched out of the hole and slid on her back down the embankment. Mud sucked the shoes off her heels, and they slapped against the soles of her feet as she ran toward his voice.

"Alek!" she yelled, pumping her arms wildly as she navigated over the uneven terrain. Tears of relief streaked her face, and she pushed through her misty vision.

"I'm here, Alek." She fell to her knees beside him. His shredded jeans revealed a deep gash in his thigh. She ripped the cord from her hoodie and passed it under his heavy leg. "This is going to hurt." She tied it into a knot and yanked on the ends.

Alek made a fist in the mud and howled in pain. "Is this what it's like to be mortal? I did not realize it would be such agony." His mouth hung open, and he breathed in shallow bursts.

"Are you hurt anywhere else?" Before he could answer, she lifted his tattered shirt. Scrapes marred his flesh, and she passed a careful hand over his torso. "You're pale. You've lost a lot of blood," she said, noticing how dark her skin appeared in comparison to his. "I thought you were like me and couldn't get hurt. How did this happen?"

His swallow was audible as he turned his neck to face her. "I had to find you. To protect you."

She took off the hoodie, rolled it into a ball, and gently placed it under his head. "You didn't need to come back for me."

He winced as a shudder passed through his body. "I believe my body is failing me."

Eva grabbed his hand and held it tightly between hers. "Don't worry about me. I have a place to hide. Go back home. You'll die if you stay here."

"My talisman. I drained it to get to you. There is no way back."

Her eyes welled up with tears. "Why would you do that?"

"Without you, our worlds are lost."

"But I can't help anyone on my own." Tears dripped onto her hands, and she released her exhale slowly to calm her shaking voice.

"I only saved you and returned so soon to reverse the curse, but I have failed. I am sorry," he whispered.

"No, you haven't failed," she said with a sob. "Everything will be okay. You'll be okay." She leaned over him and rested her head against his chest. "I don't know how to do this on my own. Don't leave me," she wept.

"You are strong. You must fight."

The amber light from his talisman flooded her vision, and Eva lifted her head. "I thought you drained all of its energy."

"Magic." He smiled weakly and closed his eyes.

"Alek, please. You can't leave me." She brushed the hair back from his forehead and slid her hand to his cheek. "I need you."

She pressed her lips against his and let the tears stream down her face.

• • •

"What do you mean you let the suspect go?" Schilling's jaw set, and he crossed his arms over his chest.

"I had no choice. There were too many people around," the female officer explained, picking crusts of blood off her hands.

"Judging by that huge puddle of blood over there," Schilling gestured to the dark slick staining the concrete behind them, "I can't believe he posed that much of a threat."

"Ease up, Schilling," James said, leaning into him. "We're here now. He couldn't have gone far."

"And you didn't see him. It was like something jump-started him. I don't know if it was shock, or what, but he was up and prepared to do whatever he had to in order to get into the park," she explained.

"Thanks for filling us in," James said, as he watched Schilling walk away mumbling under his breath. "And don't let my partner get to you. He's like that with everyone."

He jogged over to where Schilling stood staring at the trees. "Think we should split up?"

He grunted. "Be better than waiting for those jackasses in tactical."

"I grew up hiking through here. Up ahead a little ways, there's a fork in the trail. You go right, I go left?" James took his gun from its holster and clicked off the safety.

Schilling removed his and did the same. "If you find him, don't approach. Radio in your location and wait for backup. And keep your eyes open. There have been a few calls from people who've spotted mountain lions out here this year. The last thing we need is one of those nasty fuckers sneaking up derailing everything." He lifted his gun and they noiselessly proceeded into the park.

•　•　•

Eva's soft lips molded to his. She felt warm and inviting, like his first walk in the sun, and Alek surrendered to her comfort.

Heat wafted from his talisman and mixed with the newly cleansed breeze. Warm air encircled them as he wrapped his arms around her and pulled her close against his chest. Eva's heartbeat echoed through Alek like fireworks. He parted his lips and hungrily deepened the kiss.

Pain was a distant memory. His body tingled, and the heat from his crystal increased. The mushy ground vibrated beneath his back and rich gold light flooded his vision.

"Eva," he whispered, his breath mingling with hers. "Thank you."

The warm breeze shifted and strengthened. Its force kicked up leaves and debris from the ground and knocked Eva backward. Orange light flashed through the trees like fire. Large flashbulbs of light rippled in her vision, and she blinked through them, blindly searching the mud for his body.

"Eva? Where's Alek?"

She spun around. Dirt caked her hands and streaked her wide-eyed face. "Did you see that? That light. He was here. Right here. And now he's gone." Tears spilled out of the corners of her eyes.

James lowered his gun and studied her bloody clothes. "I heard you say his name. Where did he go?"

"I don't know where he went." She sucked back her sobs and stood. "I have to find him. You have to help me."

"Don't come any closer," he instructed, holding his hand out in front of his torso.

She took a few small steps forward. Pressure crept into her chest, a power inching its way in. "I know you think I did all these bad things, but I'm not guilty of any of them."

He lifted his gun so it was even with her heart. "Eva,

stay there. Don't come any closer."

Her voice caught in her throat. "W...Why are you pointing that at me? I haven't done anything."

"I said, don't come any closer." His grip tightened, and he clenched his teeth.

"Detective, please just give me a chance to explain," she pleaded. The pressure intensified, and Eva took shallow breaths against its heaviness.

James lightly smoothed his finger over the trigger. "I will shoot you, Eva. Don't think I won't."

The weight in her chest felt pinned to an invisible string tugging her back. She forced her body away from its pull. Twigs snapped under her feet as she shuffled closer to James. "Detective, listen to me." Pressure forced the air from her chest and clutched her heart. It tore through her, dragging her backward.

A crack like gunfire roared through Mohawk Park. A stink of smoke singed the air.

James lowered his pistol. "Eva?"

EPILOGUE

Amber light burst into the cave, spreading like smoke, stretching its warm rays through every alcove and fissure. Its otherworldly glow brushed recesses that had remained untouched for years. In those crevices awoke a resting wickedness. Each malevolent fleck spun to life. They hovered together and let the wind carry them from the cavern. The small specks of black drifted with the breeze. They stretched their sluggish bodies, relearning what it meant to be one, what it meant to be whole after decades of sleep.

• • •

Tyson sprinted down the familiar Mohawk Park trail. His feet pounded the ground in perfect rhythm. Blood surged through his legs, and he smiled, admiring his body's power.

"Damn gnats," he mumbled, taking a deep breath and fanning the air in front of his face. Whispers spun around him as he inhaled. "Hello?" he said, pulling one of his ear buds out. "Anyone out there?" He jogged in place and studied the still woods around him. "Huh." He shrugged and poked the ear bud back in his ear.

He prodded at the volume button on his phone, and continued his poor attempt at rapping as he jogged along the muddy trail. "When you come up from the bottom, duh duh duh duh duh duh chosen. Yeah."

He bobbed and weaved, ducking shots from his invisible opponent and landing others. He reached the end of his route and threw his hands up in the air. *And the new UFC champion is Tyson Andrews. The crowd goes wild.* He cupped his hands around his mouth and shouted in hushed tones. "Ahhhhhh! Tyson we love you!" He continued his mini celebration as he shuffled to the parking lot.

He shook out his extremities and did a few light stretches before removing the headphones and slinging the cord over his shoulder. "And what was the time for today?" Velcro scratched and popped as he removed the iPhone armband from around his bicep. He opened his running app and scanned his stats. "Not good, Tyson. Not good. Has to be all the mud. And those gnats. I hate those fuckers. Lost a good two minutes on them alone." He popped open his gas tank and fished around for his keys. Faint whispers swirled around him again, and he paused before opening the trunk.

"Hello?" He turned and looked around the empty parking lot. Dryness itched the back of his throat, and he stifled a cough. "Fucking gnats."

He popped the trunk and sat on the lip of the bumper. He peeled off his mud-caked shoes and socks, tossed them into the opening, and grabbed an old towel. Dirt stuck to the back of his legs, and he roughly wiped it away. The tingling in the back of his throat persisted, and he snatched a water bottle from the pack before closing the trunk. The discomfort cooled as he slurped the liquid. He draped the towel over the driver's seat and collapsed into the comfort of the leather.

Hello. The muffled purr drifted into the car.

"Fucking kids." He shook his head. "Shouldn't you be in school or something?" He yelled before shutting the door.

He started the car and his dashboard illuminated. "Shit, I'm late," he mumbled, glancing at the clock hovering over his preset radio choices. "I'm never going to hear the end of this." He angrily rammed his gearshift into drive, and sped onto the road. He was almost home when the tickling in his throat returned. He took another swig of water and coughs erupted from his lungs. Water spurted passed his lips and coated the steering wheel.

"Goddamnit!" The car swerved as he reached behind his back and yanked the towel free. He wiped at the dripping steering wheel as more hacking coughs forced their way up his throat. He clutched the towel against his mouth, and his torso clenched with wracking coughs.

"Oh, shit," he groaned, wiping spittle from his chin. "Where the fuck did that come from?" He dropped the towel on his lap and cleared the last strings of mucous from his throat. Small, black flecks glistened up at him, begging for his attention. He pulled into his garage, and lifted the rough towel to his face. "That's fucking gross." He balled it up and tossed it on the floorboard before climbing out of the car.

"Babe," he called as he shut the door behind him. "You're not going to believe what I just coughed up."

Hello. The hum of multiple voices floated through his ears.

He walked into the kitchen and paused, listening for the voices. "Monica?"

"I heard you. You can tell me all about it when we're in the car. After you've showered and changed. I knew you shouldn't have gone for that run. We're probably going to lose our reservation." She turned the corner and stopped as soon as she saw him. "Tyson, you look awful. Are you feeling okay?" She set her earrings down on the counter and grabbed a glass from next to the sink. She turned on the water and filled the glass halfway. "Wait a second to drink this. Let me go grab those allergy pills out of my purse." She handed him the water before heading into the living room. "It's probably pollen or ragweed, and you know how allergic you get."

His pulse thundered behind his ears, and he let her voice fade into the background.

"Here," she said, dropping the pills into his hand. "I hope you're not coming down with something. Didn't you say a few guys in your office are out with the flu?" She held the back of her hand against his clammy forehead. "You're burning up. How long have you felt sick?"

He popped the pills in his mouth and drained the glass. "I don't feel bad. I just have this—" Violent, phlegmy coughs folded his body, and he gripped the counter to steady himself.

"That sounds horrible. You need to sit down." She scooted a bar stool under his butt. "Sit before you start coughing again."

"I'm fine," he grunted weakly as he followed her

instruction. "Just need a minute." The coughing returned, doubling him over. Black specks sprayed from his mouth and peppered the countertop. "Gnats," he gasped. "They're just gnats. I ran through a bunch of them at the park." Globs of spit dripped off of his chin and onto his sweaty shirt.

"Those are not gnats, and you're definitely not fine." She rushed over to the sink and unraveled a wad of paper towels from the holder. "I'm canceling our reservation, and I'm calling the doctor. Hopefully he can get you in on such short notice." She handed him the fistful of towels, and he weakly dabbed them against his face.

The doctor. Overlapping voices sizzled and popped, their words hissing between his temples.

"Did you hear that?" he whispered, pulling the scratchy paper towels away from his face.

"Oh my God, Tyson, your nose." Monica backed away from him slowly.

He glanced at the towels. A cherry red circle glared up at him. He touched his upper lip and looked down at his hand. "I'm bleeding."

"And your eyes. You're coughing too hard. They're getting bloodshot. I'm getting the number for the doctor. Stay right there. I don't want to get sick too." She rushed out of the kitchen. Her fast footsteps hammered up the stairs.

The clump of paper towels dropped to the floor as more coughs ripped at his lungs.

I'm bleeding. The voices taunted.

"Monica," he shouted, stumbling through the kitchen and into the living room. Terror and exhaustion sped his frantically beating heart. "Monica, can you hear them? They followed me. They're inside."

They're inside. They're inside. They're inside. They chanted.

He tore at his hair and the heat behind his eyes. "Get them out!" he screamed, foam bubbling from his throat.

They're inside. They're inside. They're inside. They screeched.

"Get them out!"

"Tyson, what are you doing?"

His body twitched as he glared at her. Clumps of scalp and hair clung to his bloody fingers.

"You're really sick." She gripped the bannister and carefully maneuvered backward up the stairs. "Stay there. I'll call an ambulance."

"They're inside." Red dissected the whites of his eyes, and he spasmodically jerked as he ascended the stairs.

"That's okay," she said shakily. "I'll get someone."

Frothy saliva fizzed from between his lips, and each breath was a gurgle.

"Tyson, can you hear me? Stay there. Tyson?"

He surged up the stairs with a growl.

"Tyson!" she screamed.

THE END...FOR NOW.

To the amazing *House of Night* fans who are joining me for this next journey, thank you!

Big thanks to my wonderful agent Meredith Bernstein. Thank you for believing in me and trusting me. Without you, there would be no Kristin Cast.

CZ and Dusty—thank you for the brainstorming help and for pointing me down the right path.

Thank you, Andrew, for being my rock, my North Star, my soft place to land. It's cliché, but true. I love you.

A huge I HEART YOU goes to my fabulous Diversion Books team. Working with each of you has been a dream come true. I could not have chosen a better editor than Randall Klein. Thank you for helping me to transform each page into magic.

 Kristin Cast is a *NY Times* and *USA Today* bestselling author who teamed with her mother to write the wildly successful House of Night series. She has editorial credits, a thriving t-shirt line, and a passion for all things paranormal. When away from her writing desk, Kristin loves relaxing with her significant other and their dogs, and discovering new hobbies. This year she'll work on swimming, yoga, and adding to her *Doctor Who* collection.